THE MYSTERY OF
THE SILVER CIRCLE

THE MYSTERY
OF THE
SILVER CIRCLE

by

MOLLIE CHAPPELL

THE CHILDREN'S PRESS
LONDON AND GLASGOW

CONTENTS

CHAPTER ONE

THE OLD INN

MY NAME is Olivia Taylor—Livvy to family and
friends. I am thirteen years of age and the oldest of
five. I am also the one who writes down everything
that happens to us. Perhaps not *everything* for I
couldn't expect you to take an interest in ordinary,
day-by-day events like the short entries in brand-
new diaries . . . "Rose. Went to school. Came
home." (I suppose that is why most diaries close,
round January 6th, for that year?) Of course, I only
write up the thrilling, exciting episodes—those
worth remembering.

Sally and Richard (my sister and brother) say,
"You write them down, Livvy. You are good at
that sort of thing." Maybe this goes to my head.
Maybe they mean it to—not wanting to write,
themselves. Anyway, that is how the story of *The
Silver Circle* came to be written—a story in which
we took part, one summer, and which I can't remember, even now, without a thrill of excitement.

It was the first week of the summer holidays, and
to me they stretched ahead like a sketch book with
pages waiting to be filled with the most exciting

pictures! We didn't know what might happen, before we went back to school in September, but we were prepared for anything! We seldom went away for the holidays. Why should we when we lived in Fold, which is on the coast and a place to which other people come, every summer, for a fortnight and longer? It is one of the most beautiful places we know and we never want to leave. We enjoy every minute there, winter and summer, and are never bored, as I am afraid we have been, the few times we have been forced to spend nights away from home.

This first Saturday, Mummy told us we might choose where we wished to go and spend the day, and need not come back to the house until evening. She had told us this the night before, and we were still undecided next morning. There were so many places to choose from—all favourites!

Richard and I did most of the arguing and Sally waited for us to finish. Sally is younger than I, though at times you wouldn't think so. She has a calm, certain air about her as though she believes without question everything she says and does is correct—and that, it seems to me, is halfway to getting other people to think the same! Richard is younger than Sally and just an average boy, I suppose. Sometimes, he thinks as I do—and sometimes he sides with Sally. It is easiest of all for Richard.

We didn't quarrel, he and I—nothing so fierce—

but one suggested a place and the other carefully and at length suggested reasons why it wasn't the right, the perfect place, for so special an occasion. It was early morning and the grass on the lawn was heavy with dew. A haze out to sea (our house is on a hill, near the harbour, overlooking the Bay) promised a brilliant day.

"Too hot for the beach," Richard said, when I suggested a picnic near the rocks and a long cool swim.

"Too hot for climbing, then!" I retorted, scotching his idea—which I knew was coming—for climbing up the rocks to the cliff-top.

Sally leaned out of the window. From the ground she must have looked rather like Rapunzel with her long plaits swinging each side of her face. "We'll go to the woods," she said.

Richard and I looked at each other, all argument forgotten. Of course, *the woods*. . . .

Sally went on, taking our silence for agreement which indeed it was. "It will be perfect there. We can go by bus, so it won't be too far. The trees will shade us—it's going to be a hot day—and there's a stream for paddling——".

"*Yes!*" we said.

Emma and Noel, who were listening, looked wistful, but we decided they were too young to come with us. "Your turn will come," we told them, sounding experienced. They looked unconvinced and trailed after us when we went downstairs to breakfast. They watched us, all through the meal, hoping we would change our minds, but we didn't. We had been through the "Not for you—you are too young" stage and didn't see for a moment why *they* should be spared!

In summer, many of the people who live at Fold prefer the woods. The visitors, I am certain, don't go there often, because they can't tear themselves away from the beach! We love Farley Woods but not because we want to get away from the beach with the hundreds of visitors and the blue and the gold, the fun and the noise. We enjoy the summer season and have friends we look forward to meeting, year after year. But that day, the more we thought of it, the more attractive a day in the woods appeared.

I think they are loveliest of all in spring, when everything is green and alive, but in summer it is a cool, shady place, filled with the hundreds of sounds that go to make up a wood—birds calling and the wind in the branches and the stream running through. . . . We have discovered some treasured and secret spots, for picnicking, and a day is almost too short to spend there.

"Remote," Sally calls it—and that is the word. She is very good with words. Perhaps she should be the writer, and not I. But Sally has always wanted to draw and paint and will be an artist one day. She makes no secret of it, and is sketching or drawing, every spare minute. I am not sure, yet, what I want to do. It will have to be something to do with *people* for I like nothing better than meeting people and getting to know them. Sally says, in that case, I should be a nurse or a schoolteacher. I don't know. Richard will be a cricketer, first. Then— he, too, hasn't quite made up his mind—a detective or an engineer. He swings between one and the other, depending on whether there is a mystery to solve or a bridge un-built. I sometimes think it would be nice for him to combine all three—or does that only happen to detective heroes in books?

We asked if we might be allowed to take with us food *to cook,* not just sandwiches and buns which are too ordinary to be exciting. Mummy was inclined to frown over the " to cook " but we let Sally explain why it would be better, this way. " It will save the bother of cutting sandwiches—and it *is* a bother—thinking up fillings! If we take the— the——"

" Raw meat?" Richard suggested, helpfully.

Mummy shuddered and Sally frowned at him. " If we take something to cook, ourselves, it will be less work, in the kitchen—and *we* shall enjoy it more."

" But starting a fire," Mummy worried. " The undergrowth is tinder-dry——"

" We shan't burn the woods down," Sally said,

confidently. "Livvy and I will be very careful. We know all about fires, from Guiding."

(I noticed she very honestly kept Richard out of it. Upon occasion, when his thoughts are elsewhere —maybe solving a mental mystery or building a dream bridge—he has been proved untrustworthy.)

"*Nothing* tastes nicer than food cooked in the open," I said, and Mummy agreed. I am certain she remembered the way she and the aunts had picnicked, in the same spot, when they were our age.

We were made to promise we would be very careful to stamp out the fire, and we did this enthusiastically because we knew, now, our picnic would turn out the way we wanted.

"Just one little frying-pan and some sausage?" Sally wheedled.

Mummy laughed and gave in. What could she do against our concerted attack? She gave us the money to buy the sausage on the way to the bus, and some more food besides. (I suppose she remembered, too, about appetites being twice their normal size, out-of-doors!) We carried two bottles of home-made lemonade and a basket of fruit. Martha lent us her second-best frying-pan and told us what would happen if it wasn't returned in the condition in which we had it! Then she relented and packed a tin box full of the fudge she had made the day before.

Emma and Noel still trailed us but we remained

stony-hearted. When we went through the gate, they hung there, waving sadly. I am afraid *we* waved gaily, before we turned the corner, and, the next moment, forgot about them. Anyway, they would go to the beach soon, and forget about us. The woods were too far for them and they would be tired while we still wanted to enjoy ourselves. (You will see from this that we did not *always* go out without our little brother and sister.)

We spent some time talking to the butcher and the grocer, then we had to run to catch the bus which started from the Square. It was moving off as Richard jumped on. It would have been *awful* if we had lost it and had to wait another hour—how Emma and Noel would have crowed!

The bus took us out of town and over the stone bridge that spans the broad, slow-flowing river. From here, it turned inland, but we got off at Shepherd's Cross and started across the stretch of heath and moorland that brought us to the edge of the woods. We looked at them, as we made our way over the tussocky grass—dark and cool and inviting, like a fringe against the sky. It was already uncomfortably hot and our baskets heavy, and we looked forward to the shade ahead. (I decided the woods were the best choice we could have made for such a day, and I think Richard did too. We didn't tell Sally this. She probably knew anyway.)

Once inside, among the tall trees which grew close

together, the light filtered green and shadowy down
on us, and everything was fresh and scented. Our
feet sank into pine needles on the ground, and last
year's leaves. Birds called among the branches and,
quite near, we could hear the stream. When we
came upon it, we sat down without another word,
took off our sandals and felt the thrill that comes
when the clear cold water runs over your feet and
splashes up your legs. There is *no* feeling like it and
I think I prefer it, even, to the sea—the stream was
so *dainty,* running there, so sweet and clean. The
stones beneath were speckled brown, and the grass,
on the banks, was the brightest emerald.

We decided, when we had cooled off sufficiently,
to walk upstream to a spot where we knew there was
a circle of grass, soft as a carpet—a splendid place
to light the picnic fire and cook and eat lunch. We
were all so content we didn't talk much, but when
we did, we all burst out together, then were silent
again. It was another world from Fold and the
crowds and the beach and pier and harbour—so
that, under the spell of it, we felt different too, on
this bright summer day which here had become
green and shadowy and mysterious.

Richard collected sticks and Sally and I built and
lit the fire in the way we had been taught. Richard
didn't mind. He was eyeing the stream with an
engineer's look and I told myself that, to-day, the
detective was taking second place. "I'm going to

dam it," he said presently, and I knew I had been right.

Sally had to ask what good he thought that would do. I told her not to nag. A scheme didn't have to be a one-hundred-per-cent sensible for one to enjoy doing it! "If Richard wants to irrigate two feet of bank, let him," I said. I wanted *everyone* to be happy to-day!

"As long as he doesn't spoil the lunch," she frowned. She and I were going to search for a fern Mummy had spoken of and said she wanted. If we could find it, we should take it home, in soaking wet handkerchiefs, and plant it on the veranda on the cool, shady side where Mummy's ferns did so well.

We left Richard with stern instructions to keep his mind and his eyes on the fire and on the sausage. We threatened him with no lunch, if he burned what we had brought! (We realised that if this did happen, it wouldn't be just Richard who would go hungry—but we hoped the threat would stay with him!) It didn't. We found the ferns quickly and were on our way back when—"Burned sausage!" Sally shouted and started to run. We found Richard busily trying to scrape off the charred bits. "I was thinking of something else," he confessed.

"Not dams?" Sally said, with sarcasm, and he had to confess that it was. Then she read him a lecture about even the cleverest and most up-to-date engineers having to stop to eat but, by then, I had scraped the sausage off all the charred skin and called to them to come and eat—a certain way of stopping Sally! In spite of the accident, the sausages tasted the way we had thought they would— better than ever—there in the open. We ate Martha's fresh crusty rolls with them, washed down with lemonade. We started a discussion about *why* food tasted this way in the open air, then didn't bother with the reason but went on eating contentedly. Richard wondered if we should keep anything for *tea*! I don't know how he thinks one meal ahead, the way he does. "Fudge and fruit," Sally said, and that decided it.

We stamped out the fire and cleaned the frying-pan thoroughly, the way Martha expected. Then we washed the plates in the stream, dried them, and prepared to enjoy, each in our own way, the long lazy afternoon hours. Sally took out her sketch book and began what seemed to me to be a most difficult pencil sketch of a group of silver birch. *I* would have drawn *one*—Sally frowned over a *composition*! Still, she never takes the easy way. Richard went back to his dam, wading through the water, looking as though he were constructing, single-handed, something in the Tennessee Valley! I leaned back against a handy tree-trunk and read, for the third time, *Robin Hood*. It was the perfect choice for a day in these surroundings.

But, when Sally finished sketching, that was the end of peace and quiet for Richard and myself. Out of the corner of my eye, I saw her snap shut her book and put it away, with her pencils, in the case. But I had finished my book and didn't mind when she said abruptly, "Let's go to The Silver Circle. I'd love to see it again."

I was silent and she turned to look at me. "It's all right," she said impatiently. "Anything that may have happened there happened years ago! The stories are vague—no one knows if they are true! It's just an old ruin now, like—like the Castle. What could happen, Livvy, *by day*?"

I didn't know. She sounded reasonable and sensible but still I hesitated. She went on, "An old ruined inn—with the sign flapping . . ."

There she went, again, painting a picture with words. By saying that, you could see, clearer than a hundred longer words, the inn in the woods, empty, derelict, its windows broken, its roof leaking, the only sound and movement the wooden inn-sign creak-creaking in the breeze, faded and tarnished and useless . . . no travellers, now, leaning forward on their horses to get the first glimpse of its name, no voices demanding the host or the serving-man. Nothing save silence . . . and ghosts perhaps?

Everyone knew of The Silver Circle but few people went there. To the grown-ups there was little attraction about the ruined inn, in the woods. To get there you had to walk far in, away from the popular spots. To us younger ones, an air of mystery still hung about it, made up from loneliness, its state of decay, the stillness and silence of the wood around, and the stories we had heard, not always reputable. Nothing could be proved, but once you had seen it, the tales didn't seem to need proof. You were prepared to believe in ghosts and haunting . . .

Once, the inn must have been a thriving place when people rode through the woods from the coast to the towns beyond. It would have made a short cut, in those days, but later, a road was built—a fine, wide road—skirting the woods and linking up all the towns so that people didn't walk or ride these paths any more. Then the inn lost its custom so that whoever owned it sold up and left.

More than one family took it, after that, but they never stayed long. I suppose it was because they couldn't make a very good living there, but that wasn't the reason the villagers gave. The more romantic explanations were ghosts and haunting so that The Silver Circle was a place to be shunned. Ordinarily, of course, we scoffed at ghosts, but a *wood* is no ordinary place. At evening, when the trees seemed to draw closer to themselves, and the bird were silent, and there was no sound save your quick breath as you hurried through, it was easy to imagine that the stories we had heard *might* be true, and very easy to say, "Don't let's go past the inn.

It's just as quick the other way." A moonlit night, with the trees etched in black and silver, the stream a high thin thread of sound—it was a perfect setting for ghosts if they were looking for a place to haunt!

Then I thought of something else that had nothing to do with ghosts but which, to me, seemed even less desirable.

Sally read my thoughts accurately. "As for *tramps*," she said, "we shall be careful. We shan't go looking for danger—and we are three! We can make an awful lot of noise and scare any tramp! Oh, come on, Livvy!"

Sally had even more difficulty in persuading Richard to leave his irrigation scheme. He said no good engineer gave up in the middle, but she told him no engineer attempted to finish a job in a day, so, muttering something about girls always wanting to go somewhere else, he slung his shoes around his neck by the laces and followed us.

The path leading towards the inn was still easily recognisable—and I forgot my fears when I came in sight of it. I decided the place looked picturesque and pleasant to-day in the afternoon light. Windows that were still unbroken glittered in the sun. Ivy grew thick along the walls, and green over the front porch, and poked inquiringly into rooms through empty panes. The old hitching post had a trail of blue flowers growing up and along it, and wild flowers grew beside the front door and in the cracks of stones.

I thought it looked like something out of a Disney film—you could expect, any minute, a chorus of bluebirds or a trail of chipmunks. . . .

The old wooden sign creaked in the breeze reluctantly, painfully, as though it must have stiff joints through being so long in wind and rain. The sign—a silver-painted circle—could still be made out on the dark wood.

I looked at Sally. She was lost in a dream, staring at the inn. I suppose, as an artist, she was imagining it the way it had been, the way it could never be again—busy and filled with travellers and news and comings and goings . . .

"Quite empty," she murmured, half to herself. "Nothing but ghosts, now, in empty rooms . . ."

I didn't know what to say in reply, but Richard brought us both back to earth when he said, practically, "It isn't empty, you know. There *is* someone there."

He pointed to where a plume of smoke, thin and grey as a feather, rose straight into the blue sky. I stared, saying nothing. Sally, at my side, drew a deep breath. I don't know how she felt but to me there was nothing so frightening as evidences of life about a place you had thought deserted—a place which should be empty but which plainly was not.

A breeze blew a smudge of smoke above the roof.

Richard took a step towards the inn and I knew Richard-the-detective had taken the place of Richard-the-engineer and I wished, there and then, he had stayed at the stream, building his dam. After all, I *was* the oldest and it carried responsibility as well as a certain kind of glory. The smoke probably meant a tramp and I think I feared them more than ghosts. After all, ghosts were what you thought them up to be. *Tramps* . . .

"Come back," I whispered, fiercely, to Richard. "It may be dangerous."

He was obstinate. He is usually an easy-to-influence boy, but when he sets his chin that way wild horses won't stop him doing what he has made up his mind to do.

I looked to Sally for support but her face was creased in a frown as she stared at the inn, and I knew curiosity was getting the better of her too.

"Only a *peep*, Livvy," she said. "I must see who it is——"

"All right," I told them. "But if anything happens, don't blame me!"

"If it is a tramp, I'll be first out!" Sally promised.

"We are three," Richard said, with an attempt to comfort.

I told him, acidly, there might be three tramps too. But there was nothing I could do save follow.

Quietly, we went towards the front door of the

inn. *Creak* went the sign—*creak-creak*. I looked angrily up at it, on the point of telling it to be quiet!

The porch led on to a dim, stone-flagged passage. It was damp and cold-smelling, in contrast to the bright, warm day outside. It led directly to the back of the house and that was where Richard was making for, walking on tip-toe with his "tracking-down-criminals" look. I had to stop and peer into one of the front rooms. It was panelled, with the same worn stone floor, and large patches of damp were plain on the walls. The window-seats were rotten. I could see holes in the wood. A fine place for mice, I told myself. They could live here, undisturbed, and rear children and grandchildren. . . . Ivy trailed through the window. The room was dark, closed-up with secrets. I hurried out again after the others.

There was a heavy door at the end of the passage. It was ajar. Gently, Richard pushed it farther open. Sally and I crowded to look over his shoulder. I sniffed. I could smell something familiar but the strangeness of the place confused me so that I couldn't recognise what it was. I felt as if I were in a dream.

Then my eyes became used to the big, gloomy kitchen. It was an enormous room. Great hooks (for hams, I suppose) hung from the ceiling, and a range took up almost all one side. You could cook for a regiment in there and not be pushed for space!

Now, it was deserted, cobwebbed, echoing, where once it must have been the busiest part of the inn!

But we only gave the kitchen one glance. Standing before the range, dwarfed by its size and flanked by ovens big enough to roast a whole sheep, was a girl a year or two older than myself. This was no tramp and certainly no ghost—but we stared at her open-mouthed. She was red-haired and wore riding breeches and a cool white shirt. She whistled a tune as she stood there, holding a frying-pan over the fire she had lit in the grate. It came about one-third of the way up and she had to stoop to cook over it. It would have needed a dozen logs to fill that grate adequately!

I recognised the smell now—sausage!

CHAPTER TWO

THE GIRL FROM RHODESIA

THE GIRL would have gone on cooking, unaware that she had an audience, if Sally hadn't spoken. Richard and I said nothing. Blue smoke went thinly up the wide chimney. It looked as wide as a cavern and the girl seemed ready to disappear into it as she stooped over the small pan she held. The only sound was the sput-sput-sput of the fat and the popping of the sausage skin as she poked at them with the fork she held.

Then Sally said, in her clear voice, "Well . . .?" and it was as if a spell were broken. The stranger straightened and turned to face us, holding the pan in one hand.

If it had been I, I should have jumped a foot into the air at the shock of seeing three faces peering at me in a place I, too, must have thought deserted. I know I should almost certainly have dropped the pan to the utter ruin of the sausages! But the stranger didn't show surprise or annoyance. She frowned a little, but it cleared quickly, and I felt as if *we* had disturbed or trespassed upon *her* privacy, here in the kitchen of the Silver Circle. I must have

28

looked the way I felt—I always do—for the frown cleared and she smiled, and I liked her, there on the spot. Her face and arms were deeply tanned, more than one could expect from an English summer, even after three months at the sea, and I decided she must have spent some time in a place enjoying more sun than we did. (When I knew her story, I was proved right.)

"Come in," she said, hospitably. "Though I don't see why *I* have any special right to invite you!" I saw she was mentally counting the sausages and dividing by four. "Don't worry," I said, quickly, to reassure her. "We've eaten. Sausages, too." She looked relieved, for certainly there wasn't enough to go round. "Do start your meal," I said. "Lunch—tea—whatever it is."

She explained that she preferred to wait until she was really hungry and cook then, because she was new to this part of the country, and spent all her time exploring and getting lost. "There's so much to see, I can't bother with lunch-at-one." But she looked wistfully at the sausages she had put out on a plate and again I begged her to forget about us and start her meal. Then I remembered our tea— fruit and fudge—and put both on the table. Perhaps it would make it easier if we all ate? Richard and I leaned against one end of the table, dipping and nibbling, while she pulled up a rough wooden stool from one side of the fireplace. "Part of the original furnishings," she said.

Sally took her tea to the window and stood there, at the edge of the group, looking on. She stared hard at the girl but I didn't know what she was thinking. I believe Sally had come to think of the inn as our own especial property, that day, and was upset to find someone else there!

The girl had with her a bag filled with ripe, juicy cherries and insisted we took a handful each. They tasted wonderful and she told us they were from her grandfather's orchard.

I was eager to know her name and more about her but decided to wait until she had finished eating. I was the one who did most of the talking—Richard, now the mystery was solved, was himself again— shy and a little vague but quite prepared to be friendly.

The girl's name was Kim Randall and she was fourteen years of age. "I don't live here—this is my first holiday at Fold. As I said, I'm new to everything."

"And you find it strange?" I persisted, thinking that now she was bound to tell us where she was from.

"It *is* different from my own country. I never get used to so much rain, almost all the time."

"Not all the time!" I protested. "Sometimes

we go for weeks without a shower. Not often, though,'' I had to admit.

She laughed. ''At home, it only rains in the wet season. We get six months without *a drop*.''

''You're from Africa?'' Richard said.

''Yes. Rhodesia. I've lived there all my life, until now.''

I had been right then! She did look un-English in a way that meant she spent most of her time out-of-doors.

''Doesn't it get monotonous?'' Sally had to ask. ''All that time without water? What happens to your gardens?''

''We have wells and bore-holes. They see us through—but you have no idea how eagerly we look forward to the Rains! I think the loveliest thing, here in England, and one I can never see enough of, is the way your streams rush over the stones— fresh and clear—not drying up.''

I tried to imagine a summer hot enough to dry up our streams—but failed!

''Do you go to school in England?'' I asked. Really, it was too bad to cross-examine her, this way, but she didn't seem to mind. I think she understood that we were interested in meeting some-one from a different part of the world. She sat, lazily popping cherries into her mouth, and told us everything we wanted to know.

It seemed she went to school in London—and disliked every minute of it!

As I have said, I was certain Sally had not warmed towards this girl, the way I had. Sometimes she takes these dislikes. No one can explain them—I don't think *she* can—so we try to ignore them. But I thought it was rude of her to appear so critical and sound so short to someone who was not only a stranger to Fold but to England! How should we feel in Rhodesia? I nearly told her all this, there in front of Kim, but decided to keep it until we were alone.

"*Why* don't you like school?" Sally asked now.

Kim shrugged and said honestly, "Homesick, I guess." She explained she had lived all her life on a large ranch, in the south of the country, and she missed the life—the space, the freedom, everything she knew and liked best. She went on to describe her home, and we didn't interrupt. Her face glowed when she did this, and it was plain that she was homesick. But her mother had insisted Kim came to the same school in England where she herself had been educated—so here she was! "But only until I am seventeen!" she said, fiercely. "Then, I shall go back—*and by air*! Much as I like England—not *school*"—she explained, with a twinkle—"I'm living for the day."

"*Why?*" Sally said again, this time more coldly. In spite of what Kim had just said, I believe my sister scented some criticism of our country, and was prepared to meet it head-on.

I turned on Sally. "Because Africa is her home!" I said, forcefully. "And no one really fits in, away from home."

"The way *you* wouldn't, in Rhodesia," Richard told her, neatly.

Sally's cheeks burned and she didn't say any more. She turned and looked out of the window.

Kim said she thought the oldness and richness and tradition of Britain was wonderful—she had spent a holiday in Scotland and Wales—and she said it quickly and sincerely so that you knew she meant it. But her face only lit up when she described the ranch and the life she had left. When she spoke, she made us see her part of the country—rounded kopjes, low-spreading msasa trees over dun-coloured grass, Christmas celebrated in the Hot Season and winter in July . . . she described the cattle at the ranch and the never-ceasing round on the farm—her father and mother and four brothers, all older than herself. She missed the horses greatly, she told us, but for this holiday her grandfather had bought her a pony, and she rode in the woods every fine day.

"What do you do on wet days?" Richard asked, interestedly.

Kim laughed. "Write to the family, describing the pony." She went on, "To-day, though, I came on foot. Penny is slightly lame—or you would have known someone was here. She would be tied to the hitching post. I found the inn almost the first day I came here. It's my headquarters. I've never seen anyone else here."

"No ghosts?" Richard asked, with a look at me. "No tramps?"

Kim shook her head. "No company at all. I bought a frying-pan and borrowed some plates and a cup and saucer—and set up house!" She smiled across at us and I thought her a delightful person and exciting to know. I wished we could see more of her, if she were staying long. "All the summer," she told me. *Good,* I thought. That gave us *weeks* together . . .

After all this exchange of question and answer, I remembered I still hadn't told her our names. Hurriedly, I introduced myself and Richard and Sally. I told her where we lived and who our father was. I described the house near the harbour, and invited her to it, on the spot . . . and, on the spot, she accepted.

After an hour with Kim, it was as if we had known her all our lives. She was that kind of person, completely at ease herself, so that you immediately felt that way too. Even Sally thawed a little, though she still remained on the edge of the group. I couldn't think why she was this way—but it does happen sometimes that two people just can't get on with each other. (Though it was Sally who was being unfriendly. Kim was as nice to her as to Richard and me.) When this does happen, I suppose the best thing is that the two concerned should see as little as possible of each other. But I told myself *I* should see a great deal of Kim, if she would have me—Sally would have to go off sketching, if that was what she preferred!

We explored the inn together, peering into empty rooms, pulling back creaking doors, some of them sagging on their hinges. The inn was dust- and cobweb-filled, heavy with gloom and silence, until Richard, with a shout, sent the shadows flying and deafened any ghost that happened to lurk.

Then Sally said, "If we want to catch the bus, we had better start."

I looked at my watch. "Goodness, yes!" But I didn't leave in such a hurry that I hadn't time to invite Kim to tea, next day.

As we walked from the bus across the Square towards our house, I trailed my feet a bit for I discovered suddenly that I was tired. But it had been a perfect day. I thought back on the picnic beside the stream, the long, lazy afternoon, finding Kim at The Silver Circle . . . perhaps that was what I liked best and what rounded off the day for, as I have said, I like meeting new people and getting to know them. I said it aloud, as we turned in at our gate . . . *"I like her. . . ."*

Richard agreed but Sally said nothing.

As I thought, Mummy liked Kim and, after that first time, invited her to tea as often as she cared to come. One thing Kim never seemed to take for granted was the fact that we had the sea "almost in our back gardens", as she said. Rhodesia, of course, is land-locked and she described the long journeys by road and rail before Rhodesians caught a glimpse of the ocean—and sometimes it was years before this happened! "If *we* had a coastline," she would say, "Rhodesia would be perfect!" Then she would turn, again, and stare at the sea from the windows with an almost comical look of amazement as though she couldn't really believe it was there in front of her. "Don't you *ever* take it for granted!" she warned us. We promised solemnly this should never happen.

I think she almost preferred looking at the sea, the way it changed in mood and colour, to being in it—though she swam well since they had a pool at the ranch.

When she asked us back to her grandfather's house, we accepted, of course, but with misgivings. We didn't want to hurt her feelings and we didn't show the way we felt but we had all heard of Judge Randall and of his fiery temper! No one saw much of him in town now, for he had retired to the lonely house beyond the woods, but when he lived in Fold, he built up a reputation for fierceness. I suppose some of the tales were exaggerated but, even so, I found myself hoping he might be away from home the day we called. His new house gave him all the privacy he wanted for it had a high stone wall, a pair of watch-dogs with a reputation as fierce as the Judge himself—and now, Kim wanted us to brave all this and visit her!

"It isn't as if we were *trespassing*," Richard said, doubtfully, when we came in sight of the gates. "Though it feels like that."

I nodded. I felt more reluctant with every step . . .

Then I saw Kim waiting for us, at the gate, and the dogs frisking round her, so I decided we should at least pass through the garden without trouble.

She must have guessed how we felt for, to start with, we were impossibly well behaved as we cast a wary eye round for the Judge. We didn't see him and soon the ice thawed and we talked easily and naturally—and as loudly as ever! We played tennis on the court behind the house until it was time for tea, which we ate under the trees. Then Kim brought out an album and showed us photographs of the ranch and the family—and, of course, the horses! But there were also snapshots of dogs and cats and a pet monkey and a tame cheetah. (Richard looked for a long time at the cheetah—but said nothing!) It was plain Kim was as homesick as ever but I did hope that we, in a small way, were making her holiday here in Fold a happy one. I did understand, though, how she felt. What should I be like, forced to go to school in Africa, and longing all the time for the house on the hill near the harbour?

Later, the others wandered into the orchard—trust Richard!—but I could not pull myself away from the lawns and the flowers. The grass was velvet-soft and the dark cedars seemed to tower up, almost piercing the blue of the sky. I had never seen such glowing colours as there were in these borders. Mummy says that to get the best from a garden you must understand and consider it—since it is a living, growing thing—and I wished she were here, for whoever had planned this certainly loved flowers! I liked, too, the way they seemed to grow in a companionable, friendly way—not "in this bed because it looked right" or "in that corner because it was part of the plan".

I tried to explain this to the old gardener I met. He was squatting beside some of the brightest, bluest larkspur I had ever seen—they seemed almost to reflect in our faces as we looked at them, for I bent over too. He wore dreadfully stained trousers and a battered felt hat pulled down over his eyes which would have disgraced a scarecrow. But he loved flowers. It was in his voice and his eyes and his fingers, as he tended them. I love them, too, and we had a long talk together. I told him about my mother's hydrangeas, and the prizes she took, and the trouble she had sometimes. He told me he had heard of them and that pleased me, very much. He also said he would like to see them. I told him, cordially, to call any time. Mummy would recognise a fellow garden-lover. Maybe, they would have some tips to give each other. "Do come," I urged. "I'll tell Mummy to expect you . . ."

"You were a great success with *my grandfather,*" Kim told me as we said good-bye. I looked at her, puzzled. Then a sudden thought came into my mind and my cheeks flamed red.

"It *wasn't* the gardener," she laughed.

My cheeks still burned long after the gates had shut behind us. Richard thought it a huge joke as he ate the cherries he had been allowed to pick. But, "How did you have the nerve to talk to him," he had to ask. "I thought he was almost unapproachable?"

"I talked to him because I thought he was someone else," I had to confess. It sounded mixed but Richard understood and agreed that if I had known it was the fiery Judge Randall, I would surely have left him there with his flowers. "It was the flowers that made it easier," I explained.

We took the short cut home through the woods. It was still light and now I had decided there was nothing to be afraid of in going this way. Meeting Kim, that day, so pleasantly and unexpectedly, had successfully laid my fear of ghosts. But we were going there that evening, for another reason. It was Sally who was most eager and, looking back now, I suppose that if we hadn't gone, on this particular occasion, we should never have become involved in the story of The Silver Circle and I should never have had cause to write about what happened and of the trail that began and ended at the old inn in the woods. But I knew nothing of this on the soft summer evening when we strolled beneath the trees, thinking back on the pleasant time we had spent with Kim, listening to what Sally had to say.

"I must go there, again, *for atmosphere*," she told us, sounding grown-up and important, as she has a way of doing, and which I find particularly irritating.

She went on to explain that she had decided that her entry for the Art Competition which was to be held during the Annual Carnival Week at Fold, would be a sketch of The Silver Circle. Nothing as ordinary as cliff or bay or beach for Sally! Carnival Week was a great occasion with us and one we looked forward to all the year round! It was the great feature of our summer season, and everyone, residents and guests, joined in the fun. There were competitions for fancy dress in the monster Carnival Procession—and for the best-decorated shop in town—and floats and cars—anything that would move! There were fireworks and bonfires and dances. There were competitions for all tastes and all hobbies and an exhibition in the Town Hall. There was "something for everyone" and I am certain no one was left out. The Art Competition was one in which all entries had to be sketches or paintings of Fold or its neighbourhood. There was a large selection of beauty spots to choose from— and I suppose it was really a very good advertisement for our town's attractions. Not that Fold needed much advertisement. If many more people came to spend the summer, it might burst at the seams!

Sally said she hoped to take the judges by surprise—for she didn't think many people would think of sketching The Silver Circle. The Castle and the harbour and the old cobbled streets—fishing boats at sunrise and West Cliff at sunset—those were the well-known and most favoured entries—but, Sally argued, The Silver Circle was part of the history of Fold too, forgotten as it might be now. It was still *there*—and *she* was going to sketch it. That was why she had to study it, both outside and inside, for atmosphere.

I told her I thought it a good idea. Secretly, though, I wondered what the *inside* of the inn had to do with sketching the *outside*! Still, I suppose artists know best and because I had enjoyed myself so much at Kim's house and because I knew Sally felt out of things, with Kim and I so friendly, I determined that now I would do anything she suggested. Everyone knows artists are strange people, not to be measured by us ordinary folk! If it was atmosphere she sought, I was prepared to wait while she found it . . .

The inn looked peaceful, dreaming there in the soft evening light. This time, I walked with no nervousness towards the door and into the dark, stone-flagged passage. Sally and Richard went upstairs but I went again into the front room with the squat bow window. There was a scurry at the panelling which I knew was mice but they didn't frighten me. I stood at the window, tracing over the little panes with my finger, deciding I would have panes like these and a window of this shape, when I had a house of my own. (I went off into a dream of wondering where this would be . . . and when . . . then told myself, "In Fold, of course—where else?") The glass wasn't like ordinary glass but thick with whorls which made strange patterns of the wood and shrubs, outside. You might see more clearly through ordinary panes, but these had a magic about them. . . .

I was thinking all this when I heard Sally and Richard come quietly down the stairs—so quietly, they sounded like one person rather than two. I suppose Sally was still trailing atmosphere, walking softly so as not to disturb a hundred-year-old ghost. Then the breeze must have caught the back door, as she opened it, for it closed with a bang.

I came to myself, then, out of my dreaming, and realised it had grown darker. Shadows, round the room, were closing in on me, crouching, just beyond reach, ready to pounce, if I stayed too long. I ran out and called along the passage to Sally, thinking she was in the kitchen.

"What is it?" her voice came clearly from upstairs. So they were up there again? I thought both of them would know their way about this place when they had finished their tour.

Angry at myself for feeling suddenly frightened, impatient with them for being so obviously unconcerned and casual, I ran up the stairs. They were in the room directly above the room I had been in. Sally was examining the woodwork. I thought, irritated, that she needn't be so *thorough*—and that Richard, staring through the window with his hands in his pockets, needn't whistle in that cool way!

"Why did you come up here again?" I burst out. "I heard you come down. Haven't you found what you were looking for, Sally—or don't you recognise it? What do you find so attractive in this place, to wander over it?"

They both looked surprised at my spurt of temper. Sally stared at me. "I never came down. I've been here all the time. There's a design in the woodwork I've been examining."

But I didn't want to hear another word about her artistic activities. "Richard, then," I said, impatiently.

"Not me." Richard shook his head. "I stayed with Sally."

"But I heard someone!" I persisted. "Someone came quietly down the stairs—then the back door banged, after they had opened it." I paused. The thought came to me then, that whoever I had heard need *not* have been my brother or sister. The inn—this big, shadowy, rambling place—was a perfect hide-out for someone who did not wish to be seen, a splendid opportunity for hide-and-seek . . . Someone I did not know and had never seen had crept down the stairs and past me, softly and secretly, and on into the kitchen. The banging door had betrayed the intruder—but he or she had gone then, into the woods. Someone had hidden from Sally and Richard, in the room above, and from me below—someone who must have watched us come in but who had had no time to wait for us to leave . . .

"*Come on*," I begged. "I'm scared." I had said it—and felt better.

Sally was inclined to tease, but Richard, when he saw the way I looked, said, abruptly, "Come on, Sally. You can't see much up here anyway," and led the way out of the room. I followed him, keeping close behind, leaving Sally, I am afraid, to bring up the rear. She didn't seem to mind. As we reached the bottom of the stairs, Richard turned to me and said, "You imagined it, Livvy. You spent too long on your own in that room. The breeze banged the door and this old staircase creaks so that you imagine someone is walking down them."

I nodded. I believed what he said because I wanted to believe it. I didn't want to think there had been someone else waiting in the inn, when we entered, watching us, creeping past us . . .

Of course, it was as Richard had said—my own imagination and the breeze. I began to feel better when Sally said, sharply, "She didn't imagine it. There was someone here—in this passage." Her eyes had picked something out on the stone floor, at the foot of the stairs. She stooped to pick it up and we all bent over what she held in the palm of her hand. "This wasn't here before. It was quite conspicuous—if it had been, we should certainly have seen it in the better light."

It was a silver ring. Quite plain, rather heavy and broad, there was nothing about it to suggest it was valuable or an heirloom or antique. Sally turned it over and peered closer but there was no inscription and no initials. She tried it on. It was much too big for her finger.

"Put it down," I said suddenly.

I didn't want her to keep it. The person to whom it belonged—who had worn it, here, and dropped it—might even now be watching to see what we did ·

with it—might be outside, among the trees, following us to see which way we went.

But Sally slipped it into her pocket. Her face, when she looked up, was mischievous. "I shall take it home to show it to Daddy. Clue Number One, Livvy, to the Mystery of the Haunted Inn. Mysterious steps on stairs—a door banging—a ring dropped and found. A silver ring . . ." She was silent, her voice trailing off thoughtfully. It was Richard who knew, immediately, what she was thinking. I confess I was too frightened for riddles.

"Yes," he nodded. "A silver ring. *A silver circle*—like the ring painted on the sign-board outside."

They looked at each other, wise as two owls, so that I snapped, losing all patience, "Coincidence— and don't start making up mysteries for this place! It doesn't need it! If you aren't coming," I warned them, "I'm going home alone."

But, as Sally followed me out of the inn, I could hear her say to Richard, "It needn't be coincidence. They could all be tied up together, in one first-class mystery! The name—and this ring——"

I was halfway towards the trees, hurrying as though pursued by I-didn't-know-what. I wouldn't even look over my shoulder to answer her and tell her she was talking nonsense. I had the strangest feeling that she was right!

CHAPTER THREE

WHEN we got to the house, I said to Sally, "Tell Daddy about the ring. Show it to him. He'll know what to do."

"There's time," she said, looking curiously at me. "What's the matter, Livvy? You look different, when you mention the ring. You really were frightened at the inn, weren't you?"

"Yes," I said shortly. I couldn't explain that, for me, it is worse to be frightened of something you couldn't give a name to than anything like mad dogs or run-away horses! Sally is reputed to be the imaginative one in our family, but this time, the inn had evidently left little impression on her, save that she had discovered a design in the woodwork!

But when we asked after Daddy, we learned he had gone to a conference. "We won't bother Mummy about it," Sally said, definitely. (I knew why—because Mummy might forbid us going there and Sally had her sketch to finish.) "I'll put it safely away," my sister told me, that evening, when we got ready for bed. She looked round. "There's only the chocolate box."

47

I nodded. "Put it there. No one will know, save us."

She took up the box which, because of its pretty design and satin bow, had pride of place on our dressing-table, and in which we kept all our personal treasures. I am afraid the description is far grander than the contents for Sally said, disappointedly, as she looked through them, "Nothing *here* to burgle."

"What did you expect?" I asked. "It will be years before *we* own anything valuable—if ever!" For I cannot honestly say I can see myself strung about with diamonds and pearls—it is a most unlikely prospect!

"And if we do," Sally finished, "we shan't keep them in a *chocolate box*!" She looked through our meagre collection—a silver bangle which had been Sally's but which was now too small even for Emma—half-a-dozen charms from last year's pudding—and a string of coral. To swell their numbers, she added the broad, rather ugly, silver ring.

Then she said, to tease me, "It *is* like the inn sign. Livvy, what if there is a mystery—a hundred-per-cent Scotland Yard mystery, bound up in our old inn in the woods?"

"It isn't *my* old inn!" I said, tartly. "And whatever mystery there is, Richard is welcome to it! Good-night."

I wanted to sleep soundly, without dreams of The

Silver Circle and small silver rings. One circle, I decided, was very like another, but if Sally wanted to make a mystery she could! I wasn't going to aid and abet.

But Daddy stayed at his Conference longer than was expected, and Mummy was called away to nurse Granny, who wasn't well—and, as happens when the days go smoothly by, my anxiety over the ring grew less until, when I did think of it, it was as something my sister Sally had picked up at the old inn, probably of no great value or importance. If my conscience did prick me about not taking it to the police, I told myself Daddy would know what to do—and we just had to wait until he came home. I couldn't keep on nagging at Sally because she had found it, and really it was up to her to decide what to do with it . . . so the ring lay in the chocolate box with the other "treasures".

All Sally thought of now was the Art Competition, for she was determined to win a prize. Last year, she had been Highly Commended among a class much older than herself, but that wasn't enough for Sally. This time, she said, she was going to come *First*—and the way she said it made us almost certain that she would. She talked of nothing else, until we got tired of listening, though we didn't actually tell her this; we gave her every encouragement and felt very noble doing it, for Sally can be trying at times. We hoped she would win it—both for her sake and for the sake of what Richard grandly calls "the family name".

It was an open Competition for artists living in Fold and the neighbourhood, and there were different age limits. Sally's was "Under-Fifteen". She was still a long way under fifteen but this didn't worry her for she has plenty of what Daddy calls "self-assurance". (That is what *he* calls it.) At school, no one could touch her for her age at drawing and painting, and after a while no one tried. She was the uncrowned queen of the Art classes and Miss Meadows, who took art throughout the school, made a tremendous fuss of her and spoke of training and scholarships. No one spoke of what Richard and I might do! It was presumed we would stay at school until we were of an age to leave—then take up some ordinary but not outstanding career. Sally, we were led to expect, was the one who would add fame to the Taylor name and end up in the Academy. I must say, it didn't seem to worry her for she went calmly and coolly along her way—but Richard and I worked hard to see she didn't get a swelled head—though there wasn't much we could do, since neither of us could draw! Now, however, we had discovered another girl who, for her age, was also an excellent artist, and equal to Sally— *Kim Randall*.

That, of course, didn't help things between Sally and Kim.

In spite of the praise and the prizes she seemed to win with such ease, Sally was desperately serious about being an artist when she was older, and, because he understood the way she felt, Daddy was willing to let her start the long, hard training, and Sally had no illusions about it. She knew it would be long and hard and that, if possible, she would have to help with scholarships. But she believed, with the rest of us, that she would be famous one day, so she planned to go ahead. But I knew that all the time she was training, she would be thinking of Richard and Emma and Noel training for careers, too. We are a large family, with not over-much money . . .

Kim's family, I had gathered, were not bothered for want of money. The ranch was large and must have brought in a good income. She went to an expensive school in London, and Judge Randall, too, was rich. Not that we envied her any of this. When you meet people you like, you never give one single thought if they are rich or poor, only whether you like them and whether they stay that way— pleasant and friendly. I thought Kim one of the nicest people I had ever know and she and I were on the way to becoming firm friends. We found the same things funny and laughed over them—and we grew serious over the same things and discussed them. I visited her now, whenever she asked, for I wasn't at all afraid of the Judge.

I began to think he had accepted me too, the day he gave me a magnificent bouquet. (It was much too beautiful a collection of roses to be called *a bunch*.) "For Mummy?" I asked, so overcome I could only stand there, holding the roses, as if I were ready to open a bazaar. "No," he said. "Not this time. *For you*." I kept the roses in a vase in our room until every time someone opened the door, petals fell on the floor.

Richard liked Kim, too, and liked being up at the house, and I think the Judge was pleased we came to keep Kim company. He seemed to show it by considerately keeping out of our way!

But Sally was on the outside of our little group. I always invited her to come with me to Kim's—but when she refused, I didn't press the point. I thought it a pity she should be this way but didn't want to make a fuss about it and perhaps make the rift deeper. It was strange, though, that Sally should be with us the afternoon Kim showed us her sketches.

I had noticed two companion paintings on the wall of the room in which we were having tea, and I went closer to see them better. They were both of the wide-spreading African veld with strange rounded stones, standing balanced, one on the other, and spreading trees and grim hills, in the distance. But it was the *colour* I stared at—blue shadows, deepening to purple—a vivid sky—a tree with orange-red blossoms . . .

"It *is* like that," Kim assured me. "Nothing of the softness here in England—your grey mist and green grass, brown hills and a sea more green than blue. At home, colours are vivid. When the jacarandas are out or poinsettias—blue and vivid red—or cream and pink frangi-panni, you have no idea how colourful they are, against that blue sky! All the flowers you can imagine." As always when she described Rhodesia, she was carried away.

I agreed it must be beautiful. "Who painted these?" I pointed to the sketches.

She said they were her own work and she had brought them across, as a present for the Judge.

Then, still anxious to show us Rhodesia, she brought out her sketch-book and showed us what was in it. Slowly we turned the pages, Kim all the time describing and explaining, and, when we had finished, I had a clearer idea than from any geography book what her country looked like. She had drawn a river bed dry and empty and desolate in the winter season—a duiker* sniffing the wind—a strange grouping of cruel-looking aloes—jolly sketches of native women and picannins on a riverbank—and sombre shaded drawings of droughtridden fields and ruined crops.

A vast country, I thought it must be, one of great distances, rolling empty miles, of space and vivid colour. "Is it lonely?" I wanted to know. Kim
* Antelope

said no. The people were among the friendliest in
the world.

"The sketches are *very good*," Sally said.

I started. I had forgotten she was there. While
Kim and I had been discussing Rhodesia, Sally
must have studied the drawings, evidences of Kim's
skill. Her voice was thin, as though it were an effort
for her to say the words. I think Kim, too, understood, as quickly as I did, what Sally was thinking.
But it was no good shrugging it off, saying it was
just a hobby of hers—these sketches were mature
and very well done. They were as good as my
sister's, I thought, with a suddenly sinking heart.
Sally knew this, too. I could read it in her face. She
wasn't envious in any stupid way. Sally is much
too sincere about her work for that—but she
couldn't help but be envious when we learned the
name of Kim's teacher, in London, where she got
special lessons. "That was one of the reasons I
agreed to come over. I couldn't get the teaching I
wanted out there."

Sally rose and left us. I let her walk on her own
round the garden, for I didn't know what to say
and, anyway, she wouldn't want me to say it. I
have said it won't be easy for her to have the training she wants—and I thought now that it must be
dreadful, when the future means so much to you,
when you want to work and to be taught, not to be
able to afford the best. It was plain Kim could do

this—but she would never need to earn money by her painting, the way Sally would . . .

I resolved to be nicer to Sally, from now on, though never to let her suspect the reason why!

When Sally came back, she said directly to Kim, "Are you entering the Competition? You should. I think you qualify through staying here with your grandfather."

Kim said she had already decided to enter. She was going to sketch The White Veil, that lovely waterfall that cascaded down the rocks near the woods and which was another of our scenic attractions. "When I saw it first," she told us, "I thought I had never seen anything so beautiful. White and shining—and unspoiled by tourists."

"No teashops or deck-chairs?" I agreed. "I believe the person who owns that part of the country has strictly forbidden that sort of thing. That's why it's quiet, there. People go only to *look* at it."

On the way home, I told myself it was plain neither Kim nor Sally meant to sketch the more hackneyed beauty spots on beach or cliff . . . and I sighed, and wondered who would win.

Sally asked us to go with her, when she sketched the inn (in spite of appearing casual, she didn't want to go there alone), but when we arrived there we had to keep a respectful distance and not interrupt, by word or deed, while she worked. Richard would wander back to the dam he had started the first time we came here, but I stayed near the inn, reading or just dreaming. I found I wasn't afraid of the place in the sunlight of morning or early afternoon, with Sally sitting sketching within sight, but I took good care we left it before it got dim and shadowy. It was no place, I told myself, to be in when shadows were falling, creeping up to occupy it, for then it looked lonely and filled with secrets which could frighten and disturb . . .

And that was the way Sally sketched it. I knew, from the first glimpse I had of her sketch, that this was the best work she had done. I suppose her sketching was improving, the way she worked at it continuously, but I had an idea that the knowledge that *Kim* was also entering the competition added a spur to Sally's efforts! She didn't want Kim to win, and Kim, I thought, would have to be *very good* to beat Sally! The inn, in Sally's drawing, looked lonely and derelict and withdrawn, with the eager, growing, up-thrusting wood all round. The contrast was sharp—trees, proud and tall, with the light glancing on trunk and branch, and the shadowy, forgotten inn. Without knowing anything of it, you could read its story, there in the sketch.

I was certain Sally would get the prize and looked forward to the day when we should watch her go up to receive it in the Town Hall, and clap our hands sore. Then, when I went along to look at Kim's sketch of The White Veil, my day-dreams died away and I asked myself if it might not be someone else we should clap for. Kim's painting of the waterfall, leaping like a live thing down the rock with the sun bright on it, seemed almost to shout with gaiety and movement.

Richard, who was as observant as most, thought as I did. He would go from one to the other, then come back to me, looking thoughtful. At last, he said, "Whichever of them loses is going to take a very poor view of it."

"Nonsense!" I had to say it though I was far from certain. "They are both sensible enough and sporting enough . . ." my voice trailed away. Kim, perhaps, but our sister Sally lived for her drawing. It meant more to her than treats or parties. Kim had other things.

Though we were frequently in the woods, while Sally sketched, we never saw smoke again coming from the window, for Kim spent all her time at the waterfall. We didn't pick up any more clues either, for whoever dropped the ring must have given it up for good.

We did meet the Browns.

Richard and I were waiting for Sally to finish when the Browns walked out of the front door of the inn, looking so casual and so much at their ease, I shouldn't have been surprised if Sally had put them into her sketch, since they almost looked as if they lived there. Then—"*Strangers*"—Richard hissed. (As I have said, he is always willing to make a mystery out of anything!) I realised they were and stared harder. Richard's suspicions are catching.

"Hello there!" they called, as if they knew us and were old friends. Indeed, that was the way with them from the start. They were so easy and charming, asking our names and calling us by them, we felt as if we had known them always. They sat next to Richard and me while Sally finished what she was doing. "Don't disturb her," they urged. "Later, when she's ready, if she's willing, we may be allowed to look." (Sally overheard and, as you can imagine, looked pleased.)

"Have you been exploring too?" Richard wanted to know.

"'*Too*'? Why? Is it a favourite pastime of *yours*—old inns?" Hugh Brown laughed.

"Lately, we seem to spend all our time here, and leave the beach to the holiday-makers," I told him.

He agreed that was generous of us. "Three less on that crowded beach probably helps! No, we weren't exploring." Then they surprised us by saying they thought of *buying* the inn! They were brother and sister, back in England after many years abroad. "*Too many*," Mary sighed. "You can imagine how, in the heat and the crowds of faraway countries, we longed for something like this—

fresh green grass, streams and moss. Now I'm getting sentimental.''

We assured her it was quite all right. She could get as enthusiastic as she wished since this was one of our favourite spots too. Mary Brown was tall and fair and pretty. Hugh, her brother, was broad-shouldered and deep-voiced. We enjoyed their company. They were so friendly and pleasant towards us—no grown-up condescension. But I had to say what we were all thinking. *"Buy the inn?* Won't it need an awful lot of repairs? And that will cost . . .?''

"Don't tell me!" Hugh groaned. "There are places in so much better condition—but Mary has set her heart on it here, with her 'green grass and streams'', he teased.

"Renovating and reconstructing will be half the fun,'' Mary told us. "We don't want to live anywhere ordinary—no house-in-a-suburban-street or 'semi-detached', I mean! We had some money left us and are looking for something *quite different*,'' she explained. "I can think of nothing I would rather do than convert this old place, then live in it! It has atmosphere.''

"Livvy thinks so too,'' Richard told them. "She believes in ghosts—footsteps coming downstairs while she's alone there.''

I told him to be quiet for they were looking keenly at me and I didn't want to appear foolish.

"The more ghosts, the better," Mary said, gaily. "After all, they won't have any claims on *us*. I shall leave them alone—treat them politely if we do meet—and everything should be all right! We've lived all our lives in big cities. Now I long for something different. I want a place in the country, out of sight of everyone. When I've finished, this will be a wonderful home and so restful."

She was so sincere, so carried away by her enthusiasm that I believed her when she said she would do it. If people make homes, the way they do in magazines, from barns and windmills, why not old inns? I told her so and her brother groaned again. "We've looked at a windmill too—everything save a lighthouse! I suppose I should be glad for *that*."

"I think I shall be content here," Mary said. Then she turned to praise Sally's sketch, which pleased the artist, as it always did, for no one is too high-minded about their work to accept praise now and again! When the Browns left, I went with Mary a little way to show her a short cut which would get them back into town. Richard was showing the dam to Hugh.

"Livvy," Mary said, half-laughing, "don't tell *anyone* you met us here to-day."

If I had been Richard, my mind would have shrilled *mystery*, but, since I wasn't Richard, I just looked at her, surprised, and she explained they weren't anxious people should know they thought of coming here. "We aren't *really* certain. You see, I still have to persuade Hugh. He thinks the idea wildly impractical, and since he will be living here with me, I have to persuade him the place is attractive and worth-while and won't cost us all the money we have. I could see, by *your* faces, you were surprised. Can you imagine how my plan would sound to a really sensible grown-up? They would think me quite mad, and maybe persuade Hugh not to agree—and I really like it here. It has everything I have been looking for."

I promised not to mention it and we said good-bye. "Though I expect we shall meet many times," Mary promised, as she waved me good-bye. When I got back to the others, I discovered Kim was there, and Richard had come back before me and already told her of the newcomers and of their plan to buy and renovate The Silver Circle. Kim, I could see, was sceptical. Evidently, this was what Mary had meant.

"Why should anyone want to buy a ruin like this —even a millionaire?" Kim scoffed. "If you were left a fortune, doing-up a place like this would swallow almost all of it! The doors are falling down —the woodwork is rotting—the place isn't *safe*! And where will you get maids, to-day, to work in that barn of a kitchen?"

"Well, it doesn't concern *us*," Sally began, but I rushed in to keep the peace. "There may be another side to them not wanting anybody to know. They may not wish whoever owns it to know how keen Mary is—or the price might go up!" I surprised—and pleased—myself with this piece of reasoning. Sally and Richard nodded. Kim remained obstinate. "It doesn't make sense to me, Livvy."

"Well, they seem very nice," I said, soothingly. "Not stiff and grown-up and unapproachable. They are young—and full of fun—the way *I* should like to be, when I'm grown-up—*not grown-up*——"

"You're contradicting yourself," Sally told me as I had known she would.

"I know," I sighed. "But it won't happen. I shall probably grow very old, *very soon,* through being head of *our* family!"

That scored two points off Sally!

When Kim stopped laughing, she said, "Well, if they decide to come here, good luck to them and to the army of painters and plasterers and decorators and carpenters they will have with them!" Then she said, looking round, "They'll have to open up this old road, Livvy—the place is becoming a public thoroughfare!"

I was to remember her words, next day, when we met another stranger!

Richard came rushing through the trees, shouting as he came, "A caravan—a super one! I only came on it by accident. It's hidden away about a mile from here. I'd love to go in. There wasn't anyone there—I prowled round a bit."

We tried vainly to shush him.

"What are you flapping your hands for?" he asked. "And don't make faces. Speak up!"

"Very well," I said. "The gentleman who owns the caravan—he's told us he does—is sitting next to Sally, sketching the inn, and has heard every word you said!"

But the stranger told my red-faced brother that, any time that it suited him, they would go back together and he would be most pleased to show Richard the caravan.

I wondered why Sally didn't mind being joined by a stranger who sat quite close and occasionally even dared address a remark to her which was more than we were allowed to do. But artists must feel differently towards each other for she answered amiably and even offered advice. He certainly needed it for he wasn't much of an artist! He daubed on a few colours which didn't look much like the inn, then gave up and decided to explore. *Why* was it, I asked myself, sitting in the sun with my back against a tree, warm and content and *safe,* that everyone felt the desire to go *inside* The Silver Circle? The atmosphere there, of age and secrecy, must reach out and touch them, inviting them in . . . The stranger came out, looking pleased and satisfied, and, deciding he had done enough painting for one day, packed up his easel and brushes, then sat beside Richard and talked cricket.

I heard him say he had been in Australia when they played the last Test. I don't know about the last Test but certainly it was the last straw, and broke down all barriers—Richard took him to his heart for ever! I wasn't bored, as I listened to the steady stream of talk—players and scores and styles and record innings—for we are a cricketing family, but suddenly I noticed how, while he talked, the stranger kept slipping in questions about ourselves and our friends—how often we came here—did we ever meet anyone or was it quite deserted? Impatiently, Richard would reply, anxious to get back to Australia. But I did think how inquisitive the stranger was—what on earth had all this to do with painting the inn?

The afternoon wore on. He had a picnic tea, in a basket, and generously invited us to share it. Even Sally stopped work for the day, and joined us. It should have been fun and Richard, I know, found it so, but I couldn't shake off the feeling that something was wrong—somewhere. There was nothing about the stranger you could take exception to—he was as friendly and as charming as Kim or the Browns, both of whom we had met here—but I think it was the fact that we had met yet another stranger, here at The Silver Circle, that gave me this undeniable feeling of suspicion and distrust. Visitors came to the woods and strolled round to look at the inn if they were near it, but I had never before heard of anyone wishing to buy it nor of someone wasting time painting it, when he was obviously not an artist, and looked far more pleased when he had spent some time inside exploring it. What was here, suddenly to attract strangers? Kim, I knew to be innocent of motive but I could not rid myself of the feeling that something here was not as it should be, in spite of the picture the inn made, with the wild flowers and grass growing beside the front door, and the sun shining on it and on the trees.

I rose and went towards it but did not go inside. Instead, I walked round the corner of the building and along one side towards the tangle of shrub and bush and overgrown plants where the kitchen garden must once have been. At that moment, I felt very much alone and, because of it, miserable. I told myself I must feel this way because Sally thought only of her sketching and because Kim was a long way off, and no company, and Richard even farther off, with a stranger, in Australia. I felt disgruntled because I was alone—but I wished I could shake off the feeling that around the corner something waited, ready to pounce!

I passed between gnarled old trees. They would do fine, I thought, for illustrations to the more unsettling fairy-tales. (Was the stranger still there, talking to Richard, slipping in his questions?)

I muttered, aloud, "I'm sure he isn't an artist."
"He isn't," a voice said behind me.

I turned. Then, "Don't be frightened, Livvy."
It was Mary Brown. She slipped from between the trees and came to stand beside me. I saw that she looked pale, as though *she* were frightened. I almost said this.

"I heard your voices, in front of the inn. I was going to join you, when luckily I saw someone else there."

"*Luckily?*" I repeated. "You mean the man with the caravan—the artist?"

"He isn't an artist," she said again, slowly, so that I knew she was speaking the truth.

I stared at her. We stood hidden even from the inn by over-grown bushes. They seemed to press in on us like some wild, enchanted garden, and I shivered. I thought of the three figures sitting in the sunshine on the other side of the inn—of Sally and Richard not knowing to whom they spoke. Here, I knew, was the fulfillment of the strange, haunting feeling I had had all afternoon. I found I didn't want to be told who he was nor why he was there. I didn't want a mystery to be made of this echoing, deserted place which was so fitting a background for mystery. But I had to listen to Mary. What else could I do when we stood there, together, and she was speaking of a stranger who had arrived suddenly from nowhere to join us at the inn—a stranger who had the power to make her look frightened and bitter in a way I had never seen.

"What did he say his name was?" she asked, in a whisper.

"I don't know."

"It will be a false name. Livvy," urgently, she put her hand on my arm, though I knew she did not know she was hurting me by holding it so tightly. "Livvy, don't tell him about Hugh and me. Don't let Richard or Sally tell him, ever."

"You know him well, then?"

"We know him," she said. "We have cause to know him. I believe he is here because, in some way, he has tracked *us* here. We can never feel safe from him. I thought, this time, we had slipped away—that was why I wanted to buy this old place —to feel secure."

"But he found you?" I said, speaking like some-one in a dream.

"He has followed us half-way across the world," she told me.

CHAPTER FOUR

A MYSTERIOUS BURGLARY

MARY didn't tell me any more at the time. She left, slipping between the bushes and so out of sight, and I went slowly back to the trio at the front of the inn. I tried to behave as though nothing had happened —as though I had not met Mary Brown nor heard what she said about the stranger—though it was hard to do this when Richard enthused, all the way home, about his cricket knowledge and Sally agreed that, though he knew little about Art, he was a very nice person . . .

The next day, Mary told me more. I met her on the beach where I was poking about in pools, which has always been my especial delight. Her brother wasn't with her and she looked lonely, sitting there staring out to sea. I remembered how she had told me they had lived all their lives in cities and how she longed for a settled home. I had thought she would stay in Fold now, and be happy here with us, but after what she had told me yesterday, they might have to leave again—perhaps that was what accounted for the way her shoulders seemed to droop.

I was beside her before she noticed me. "Hello!" I said.

Quickly, she turned. There was no need to look so frightened, I thought. Evidently, she had been far away. She looked, at that moment, quite different from the person I knew—not only frightened but, when that passed—angry. I apologised, and, "It's all right, Livvy," she said, trying to smile. "I was thinking of something else. Why aren't you at the inn? I thought *that* was your favourite spot?"

"I've been neglecting the beach," I told her. "But it is Sally and Richard who prefer the woods. Sally espccially. I suppose it is a wonderful place for artists." I stopped, uncertain whether I should go on. I knew we were both thinking the same thing . . . the mysterious "artist" who had appeared there, only yesterday.

Mary looked out to sea, her eyes narrowed. "*He* is no *artist*," she said again.

I thought we had bettter get this cleared up, once and for all. "Who is he, then?" I asked boldly.

"He worked for my father, once, in South America, when we lived there. Father trusted him in a position of responsibility. I won't bother you with details but there was money involved. Hugh and I distrusted him but Daddy wouldn't hear a word of it, until the end came, and he was proved to be what we said he was. My father put great trust in people, always. Hugh was responsible for proving the man's guilt and, of course, there was nothing to do save dismiss him. But, ever since that happened, I have felt frightened. He is a vindictive person and I am certain he is thinking up some kind of revenge. We have seen him in two places, since that time. Once in Sweden and once in Australia."

"He told Richard he had been in Australia."

She looked swiftly at me but said nothing. I tried to sound comforting. "But he can't do anything, here in England."

"You don't know him. He has patience and he will *never* forgive us for finding him out." Then she said, urgently, "Livvy, Richard and Sally won't tell him about us being here?"

"I don't think so," I said. It had been difficult, without sounding mysterious, to ask my brother and sister not to discuss the Browns with the "artist" who had suddenly appeared among us. When I tried, the evening before, Richard said, bluntly, "Why not?" and I had to give a reason which sounded weak, even to me. I told them Mary and Hugh had known him, somewhere else, and didn't want to meet him again. Richard looked dubious but Sally, evidently understanding that you could take a dislike to people, agreed. "That does happen," she said. "All right, I won't mention them."

Richard muttered something about "Who would want to talk about strangers buying old inns when they might discuss the M.C.C. and Test Matches?"

"*They* won't say anything," I said again, to comfort Mary.

"He may not have seen us," she said. "We *must* keep out of his way. If he isn't *certain* we are here, he may go away."

I didn't tell her what I was thinking—that the stranger must have known they were here or he would not have turned up at this lonely place which wasn't a spot much frequented by people who didn't know the district.

"Will it stop you buying the inn, now?" I asked, regretfully, for I liked her so much and looked forward to taking a hand in the reconversion of The Silver Circle—and to being a frequent visitor, when they were installed. She said she didn't know and I stopped asking any more questions because I could see she was upset. I thought it dreadful to be followed and frightened, this way.

When Kim asked me what had happened to the people who wanted to buy the inn, I told her vaguely the outline of Mary's story. I didn't go into any details of what Mary had told me on the beach, but I told Kim at least as much as Sally and Richard knew. For one thing, I wanted Kim to keep abreast of what went on in our part of the wood—and again,

I told myself, if ever the time came when Mary might need help, I should feel much better if I had Kim at hand. I told her Mary Brown and her brother were trying to keep out of sight of a stranger who had turned up and who had known them once. It sounded lame and Kim, as I had feared, was sceptical so that I wished I could have told her everything.

Her mouth seemed to button up whenever I mentioned Mary Brown, for Kim had never been able to accept the story of wanting to buy and live in The Silver Circle. To her, it didn't make sense and no story about Mary wanting to end an exile by living here in an English wood made much impression. She listened now, to what I had to say, then said, herself, ''She certainly likes to surround herself with mystery! I wonder what the *other side* of the story is?''

I had nothing to say to that.

But the stranger whom Mary disliked and even feared had a strong ally in my brother Richard. Richard never did mention the Browns to him but he never left his side when the ''artist'' appeared with his easel before the old inn. No one who liked cricket nor described it so well—''the finer points of the game,'' as Richard loftily said—could, in any way, be suspect. ''I shan't stop seeing him— not if there are fifty strangers who don't like him!'' Richard said flatly.

So he went on being a shadow of Peter Blake, who came each day from his caravan to waste time trying to paint a picture—for even Richard had to admit, cricket notwithstanding, Mr. Blake hadn't much idea of perspective!

The stranger agreed cheerfully that he would never earn a living as an artist and I wondered what he did earn a living at. Once, I even asked him this but he only said, with a warm smile, that at the moment, he was on holiday.

"He will never get a prize!" Richard said sadly.

"He isn't doing it to get a prize," I snapped, adding what perhaps I should have kept secret. "It's a cover to watch the Browns and the inn. The Browns don't come here, at all, now."

"*Rot!*" And Richard stalked off.

"If you knew all," I thought, darkly, "you wouldn't be so certain of your *Peter Blake.*"

But, if possible, Richard stayed closer to him than ever, after that—probably to make up for my doubts!

Sally was completely taken up, as Sally always was, in her Art!

Then I decided to forget these cross-currents and suspicions and to ask Kim if she knew of the cave beneath the water-fall. She hadn't heard of it so I offered to show it to her—and to take the afternoon off from Sally and Richard!

The cave wasn't dangerous, exactly, but it was

a place Daddy didn't want us to visit alone, but
didn't forbid because he never thought we would go
there. (That is a piece of reasoning I have always
found useful.) But our parents were still away and
I told myself I would be careful, so why ask Martha's permission? So Kim and I went off.

I don't suppose many of the casual summer
visitors knew about the cave. It was a secret *we*
had hugged to ourselves since Daddy told us *he*
hadn't shown it to anyone since he and his brothers
climbed up and down, when they were young.
There was no path down to it. The river banks were
steep here, and high, and in wet weather it was
impossible to go down—you would slither until you
ended in the water! Kim and I hung on to the
shrubs and stout ferns that grew thickly down the
bank. No one saw us because we went away from
the head of the fall to make our start. The loose
stones beneath our feet were treacherous, and when
they fell we could hear the splash into the water.

We came to the bottom and stood, getting our
breath back, on the flat, worn stones. "Jump
along," I said, "until you come to that ledge.
Climb up on to that and you are *under the fall*!"

I had to shout to make myself heard. The White
Veil is not a big waterfall—not by the standard of
the Victoria Falls which Kim had seen and described
to me—but, when you were as close as this, it
sounded like a train rushing by.

We jumped from stone to stone, getting wet up to our knees, until we came to the ledge, then we clambered on to it, and edged across until we stood together on the glistening wet rock, while in front of us the fall flung itself out in a white arc, sparkling with hundreds of points of light, bright as diamonds, where the sun glistened on it.

It was a beautiful sight and Kim could hardly keep from dancing with delight at being there. "Livvy, it's wonderful! We should sit on the rock, combing our long yellow hair, beguiling travellers. I feel wet enough for a mermaid."

"Travellers don't need beguiling," I said. "Not when they have the beach and the tea-rooms. Besides, you don't want a *crowd* here, do you—like The Silver Circle?"

Then she said, "But where is the cave?"

I led her back along the ledge, directly beneath the water. We got wetter than ever and our hair stuck damply round our faces. The mouth of the cave was simply a hole in the rock—dark and damp and particularly uninviting while the sun shone on the water and there was a rainbow over our shoulders! Kim grimaced and said one would have to be a frog to enjoy that dark and damp, and who wanted to be a *frog* when, at the same time and in the same place, one could be a *mermaid*? Another afternoon, we planned, we would explore the cave. I think we were both glad to put it off. (We didn't know, then, under what circumstances we should come back—nor how we should feel—nor all that would have happened, in the meantime. Just as well, too!)

We climbed up the bank again, and greatly surprised two elderly visitors at the top, who stood admiring the view. They must have wondered exactly where we came from, suddenly rising like that, then casually walking off! We left them vainly searching for a path down.

An afternoon spent with Kim always made me feel contented and happy so that, when I reached home, I didn't grumble that it was Sally's turn (as it was) to help with supper. "They aren't back yet," Martha said. "Sometimes I think we should strip this house and set it up in the woods!"

Now that Granny was better, Emma and Noel had gone off to join Mummy, so that we were a smaller family. We were quite safe, though, with Martha. She has been with us as long as anyone can remember and is very much one of the family. She rules us with a rod of iron but can be kind when you least expect it, and when it helps most.

I was halfway through laying the table when Sally and Richard came in. "You're late!" Martha snapped. Then, before they could say anything, "Richard—a clean shirt! Sally—change your frock!"

They knew they shouldn't start supper until they

were as presentable as Martha wished, so, with backward glances at the table, they trailed upstairs. "I'll do your turn to-morrow," Sally told me, and I nodded. She would indeed.

Richard was down in three minutes. His hair was slicked back, his face shone, and his shirt was gleaming white. Martha looked at him and nodded.

Sally took much longer. Richard stood eyeing the strawberry shape and muttering about girls "titivating".

I went upstairs to tell Sally to hurry, and Richard, unable to bear looking at that forbidden feast, followed on my heels.

Sally hadn't changed. I was on the point of saying, "Whatever is the matter—you are holding everything up——" when something different about the room made me stare and say nothing. It was unlike my neat, methodical sister to leave a room in this state. It had been tidy when I came up to change for supper. "What have you been doing?" I asked, indignantly.

"It was like this when I came in."

"Well, I didn't do it!" I snapped.

The drawers of the dressing-table lay open and handkerchiefs, ribbons, scarves and socks were on the floor. Frocks were half in and half out of the bottom drawers, our shoes lay about as though they had been kicked in haste and had skidded across the room: our one hat apiece lay on the floor beside the bed. I couldn't understand it. It wasn't Sally. It wasn't Martha nor I . . .

"*A burglar!*" my voice croaked and didn't sound natural. That ugly word! Applied to our house!

"Well, he chose the wrong room," Richard said. "No family jewels here." For once, he seemed amazed at what had happened. Evidently, this was bringing detection too close to the family . . .

There weren't many jewels in the house, save Mummy's rings, which she wore, and some earrings and necklaces. But when Richard said *jewels,* something clicked in my mind. I turned to the dressing-table but Sally said quietly, "That was what they wanted, I think. The silver ring. It's gone."

We stood as if turned to stone. I had the feeling which had haunted me at the inn, of being mixed up in something ugly, something better left alone. There was no one we could tell. Daddy and Mummy were still away and if we told Martha, there would only be one reply, "You are not to go near *that place* until your father comes home." Sally hadn't finished her drawing and had to go back. I knew she was thinking of this as she looked at me, almost pleading with me not to tell Martha. "We had better keep quiet about it," I said weakly. Sally looked relieved. "But who——?" I began. Then I glanced at Richard. His face was scarlet. I thought I knew what he was going to say and I was so upset and frightened, I wasn't going to let him off. "What is it? Did *you* tell someone Sally found a ring on the floor of the inn?"

He nodded.

"Peter Blake?" I said. This time he didn't have to nod. You could see it in his face.

"*When* did you tell him?"

"This afternoon."

"But you've been with him, all the time, haven't you? He wouldn't have time to come here. You stick so closely to him."

"He went off," Sally said. "He said he had had enough painting for one day. He lent Richard a book and we never saw him afterwards. Richard and I have been on our own all the time. You were with Kim. There was no one at the inn—not even the Browns." Then she frowned. "But how would Peter Blake know where *my* room is?"

"I told him it was at the back, over the veranda," Richard confessed. "I told him you had the ring safe in your room, waiting to show it to Daddy."

"You didn't have to tell him," I interrupted. "I expect he asked you questions, the way he does, and, before you knew it, you were telling him everything he wanted to know. He's clever that way."

Richard didn't argue but went on with his story. "I told him how easy it would be for anyone to burgle our house! You could easily climb one of the columns of the veranda and through a bedroom window. Martha, being deaf and probably in the kitchen, wouldn't hear anything. 'Now would be the time,' I told him, 'with Mummy and Daddy away, and we three out all day. Even Emma and Noel aren't around to watch. Anyone could burgle *anything* in our house,' I told him. 'Only there is nothing to burgle—nothing valuable.' I told him that—really I did!'"

"He couldn't have taken your word for it," I said with sarcasm.

"He asked if a burglar wouldn't be seen from the houses around," Richard said, doggedly supplying us with all the conversation, "and I said no—the trees would screen him."

"You told him all that?" I asked. "You didn't leave him much to find out for himself, did you?"

"I didn't tell him about the ring being in the chocolate box," Richard said, "because I didn't know where it was. You didn't tell me. I just told him Sally had found the ring and taken it home."

"If you don't come down, *at once*," Martha's voice came wrathfully up to us, "supper will be cleared away—*all of it*!"

But even Richard didn't look hungry, now. He looked upset and miserable. "Peter Blake didn't seem interested in the ring. He just asked if we thought it was valuable and what we had done about it. Then we spoke of—of . . ."

"The easiest way to get into the house?" I finished for him.

"I didn't tell him *where it was*!" he added, defiantly, as though that excused everything else he had told him!

"No," I said. "He had to search until he found it—and he isn't a tidy searcher!"

CHAPTER FIVE

THE MAN ON THE CLIFF

THE next day, neither of us had much to say about the disappearance of the ring. It was as if, for different reasons, we each decided to remain silent. Sally didn't want anyone to know because she still had visits to make to the woods to complete her sketch. Richard was quiet because, I think, that way he hoped we would forget the part Peter Blake must have played in it. I found *I* couldn't forget it easily though I, too, didn't wish to speak of it. It was an almost unbelievable thing to happen to *us*!

I did know that Daddy would be angry, when he came home. He would say, "Why didn't you tell me at once?" and when we gave our lame excuses, would add, "Someone in authority, then?" I knew that was what we should have done and that my first feeling about the ring had been right—it was sinister—otherwise, why should whoever was looking for it have taken such risks to get it back? If they had been caught climbing the pillars of our veranda to force an entry into the house the consequences would have been serious. Yet they were willing to do this and to search for the ring. It didn't look valuable but it must have considerable mean-ing for some person.

I told myself it must be Peter Blake—and the story Mary Brown had told me about him stayed in my mind so that I decided he was a person it was best to see little of. I wondered if I had enough authority with Richard to order him to do just this?

"Are you going into the woods?" I asked Sally, at breakfast.

She said she had to go that day. "I'm finishing the sketch."

"Take care!" I warned her, darkly. Then I turned to Richard. He was waiting for me to speak but when I drew a breath, prepared to argue, he said quickly, "All right, Livvy, I won't go into the woods. I'll go anywhere you say."

I was taken aback but didn't show it. *"Good!"* I said, and tried to think of a place far away from woods and inns and mystery. I sat there, scowling and thinking, when Martha came into the room. She must have known what troubled me because she asked if I would take a message to Mrs. Letty. Martha's messages to Mrs. Letty were famous in our family. Backwards and forwards they went, throughout the years, and we had given up count-ing how many we had delivered! Strangely enough, they always seemed to come when they were most needed—when we were fretful or didn't know where to go—when it was raining, even, and we couldn't go to the beach but could brave the five miles to Mrs. Letty's farm! Then, Martha always remembered a message.

I suspected she waited until just these times before telling us she wanted a message taken but we were always delighted to oblige. She said, now, looking from one to the other, "Which of you will take a message to Mrs. Letty?"

"Richard and I," I said promptly.

Martha said she wouldn't be a minute, writing a note. I told her not to hurry. Then I looked at Richard and my expression said, plainly, "There —that takes care of that!" and his expression said, "All right—I'll come with you, to-day. But to-morrow, I shall meet Peter Blake again."

To-morrow, I thought, could take care of itself. To-day, if I had it free of woods and inns and mystery, would help me to face To-morrow.

Mrs. Letty's farm was along the coast. Her husband was dead but she carried on alone, helped by her cousin whom we, and everyone else, called Jed. Mrs. Letty was stout and jolly and her face creased with laughing. Jed was tall and thin and took not a dark but a *black* view of everything. Sometimes, I wondered if Jed didn't depress Mrs. Letty but Martha said he was a good worker and Mrs. Letty didn't listen anyway . . .

The message was written, sealed in an envelope and given me with strict instructions to hand it to

Mrs. Letty herself, or Jed. There was no one else to hand it to—and I had given Mrs. Letty many messages in my time, but I took it as though it were a diplomatic document and I a secret and confidential courier, tucked it safely into the pocket of my dress and said no one save Mrs. Letty should get it. "What time shall we come back?" I asked. "Stay for tea," Martha said. This was unnecessary, too. We never did anything else.

The bus took us to within a mile of the farm, then we walked along a dusty road until we came to the stile, climbed over it and wandered along the edge of the big field until we came in sight of the farmhouse, tucked away beneath the hill. It looked like something in a fairy-tale, Mrs. Letty's farm, with the white-washed walls and sloping roof and hollyhocks growing like sentinels. There was a flagged path to the front door and a hen with chicks and a cat with kittens—we loved every part of it and every minute we spent there. It seemed as though it dreamed the years away, tucked away here out of sight, and that what was happening in the world outside could not touch the Letty farm. I hoped it would go on this way, and that when I was old—quite old—I could come back and walk up the path and find Mrs. Letty as she was now, smiling her welcome at the door, ushering us into the kitchen from which came the most delicious baking smells.

We started immediately on what was offered us —fresh crusty bread and farm butter and two great beakers of milk. We never apologised here for the size of our appetites! This was a snack, Mrs. Letty said, "something between breakfast and lunch." She didn't expect it to interfere with a real meal at one o'clock! I once asked her what it was that made us hungry, always, at the farm. She said she didn't know but, whatever it was, it had been there when she was a girl and she supposed it would always remain.

Jed was as taciturn as ever but that didn't stop him from eating well, I noticed. After the meal, Mrs. Letty suggested we went down to the beach "to work up an appetite for tea." That would give her time to cook something special for us! Jed was driving out to see a neighbour so we went part of the way with him. He dropped us at the corner and we waved until he was out of sight though we need not have bothered.

"What makes him so miserable, do you suppose?" I asked.

Richard didn't know. He thought Jed must have been born that way.

"Richard," I began. Then I stopped. He looked at me, so I went on, "I couldn't help it—it was lying open, on the table, and you know how you read something, sometimes, almost without taking it in?"

"*What* did you read?" Richard asked.

"Martha's 'message'. It said, 'The children need a day off. Hope you are keeping well. Call when you are in Fold. Affctly. Martha.'"

We looked at one another. For years, we had been carrying "messages" from Martha to Mrs. Letty. For years, we had hurried to get them delivered, thinking they contained something of breathtaking importance. For years, we had enjoyed the day at the farm . . .

"Don't let Martha know—ever!" I warned. "*She's a dear!*"

We went, singing *Shenandoah,* down to the beach.

This was no beach like Fold, with a wide golden curve and swimmers and paddlers like a fringe on the edge of the water. The beach here was bleak, shingle-covered, the cliffs behind rising almost sheer. I wandered among the rock pools at the far side of the beach. They were fascinating and I poked and pried and peered. I lay flat and stared a crab in the face. I heard Richard cross the shingle towards me and make a fine noise on the stones. I nearly called to him to be quiet—then the noise stopped and I was glad for the crab seemed to prefer silence . . .

Then, "*Listen!*" Richard said, as the crab and I were getting acquainted. "Someone calling!"

I sat up and looked round. "I can't see anyone."

"I can't *see* him," Richard agreed. "But I can
hear him."

I listened harder . . .

"It's up on the cliff," Richard said. "Someone
must be hurt, climbing."

I wanted to ask why anyone should wish to climb
such dangerous-looking rocks but decided to waste
no time talking. Richard started running across the
shingle and I followed. Stones slipped and shifted
beneath our feet. We began climbing. We had to
cling on to jutting pieces of rock and wriggle
between crevices and over boulders. It was hard
going but the calls for help, which I could hear more
clearly now, spurred me on. *"He-elp!"* They
came faintly down to us. Then there was silence.

"Are there passages here?" I asked Richard, as
we passed what looked like the entrance to a cave.

"I think so," he said. "Relics of the old
smuggling days perhaps? But he isn't in a passage.
I can see him—on the ledge, there. It's broken his
fall."

The rocks seemed knife-edged, as we climbed
over them. I tore the hem of my dress but didn't
stop to wonder what Martha might say. All I wanted
was to get quickly to the injured man. But when
we did see him, I nearly cried out in panic. He was
unconscious, his shirt torn from the fall, his face

ashen and a cut bleeding from his forehead. I felt helpless and more than a little scared. The ledge was wide enough for us to stand easily, but I decided *not* to look down. Richard bent and touched the man and he moaned a little. He couldn't have been there long, I thought, for the blood on his face hadn't dried. I tried to wipe some of it off with my handkerchief but my hand trembled. Then I thought of what might have happened if the ledge had not broken his fall . . .

Richard was more practical and more useful than I. "We must get help, Livvy." (Sometimes, as in the case of the burned sausages, he can exasperate by his dreaminess but he is what is known as "good in times of crisis.") "We can't do anything on our own. He is too heavy for us to lift and we may do him an injury. One of us must climb to the top of the cliff and see if there is anyone on the road. If not, we must go to the farm." He looked at me and saw the way I was. "*You* go up," he said. "I'll wait here with him. But hurry!"

I was on my way up before he finished speaking. Having something to do, I find, is always better than sitting around, and I was grateful to Richard for knowing this. I should have hated to stay there with the injured man. I climbed as fast as I could to the top of the cliff, collecting many scratches and bruises myself. When I got there, I ran across the grass until I came to the road down which we had ridden with Jed. There was no one in sight and I supposed I would have to run all the way to the farm and ask Mrs. Letty for help. Then I heard the sound of a car behind me—and there was Jed! "Lost your brother?" he asked, unhappily. I told him no—and described what had happened, on the cliff.

"Nasty place for accidents," Jed agreed, getting out of the car. "Silly to climb there—asking for trouble." But, all the time he was talking, he hurried with me to the top of the cliff. Before we could start climbing down, Richard's head came up over the top. This surprised me so much I couldn't say anything but just stood there, pointing my finger at him. We must have looked very stupid—Richard, his face white, only his head and shoulders appearing over the top of the cliff and I standing pointing accusingly at him. Now Richard didn't look the way he had looked when we first came upon the injured man—surprised but able to deal with it. Now he looked as if he had come upon something he wasn't capable of dealing with.

"Why have you left him?" I said, sharply. "You should have stayed until we came back."

Richard found his voice, then, though it came cracked and shrill. "*He's gone!*" he said.

"*Gone?* But he can't have gone! He was unconscious. He couldn't move!"

"He's gone!" my brother repeated. It seemed

all he could say. Jed, unexpectedly, was kinder than I. He saw the way Richard's hands were shaking. He leaned down and pulled him up on to the grass. "Take your time," he said.

I didn't want Richard to take any time. I wanted him to tell his story. I wanted to go back down the cliff face and look for the injured man for I could not believe he had gone. Gone where? How could he get up and make off in the state we had found him—bleeding and unconscious? Impatiently, I listened to what Richard had to say . . .

He had been sitting beside the man, waiting for me to return with help, when he heard the sound of someone scrambling down the cliff-face, to his left. He couldn't see anyone, because the rocks jutted out there, but whoever it was made a great noise of loose stones and shingle, dropping down. Richard shouted for help but there was no answer, so he decided to climb across and see if he could find whoever it was and explain that he wanted help. The rocks made a fine place for hide-and-seek and he spent some time searching, especially as he lost a shoe and had to search for that too.

"It couldn't have taken all that time," I said. "It's only fifteen minutes since I left and found Jed and came back."

Jed came to Richard's aid by saying that fifteen minutes, here on the cliffs, could seem like thirty. I considered Jed was most unfairly aiding and abetting Richard but I said nothing save, "Well, what did you do when you found them?"

"I didn't find them. I called and looked but they must have gone down to the beach, out of hearing. The wind may have carried my voice away."

"That's funny," I had to say. "We heard the injured man quite easily, and he wasn't calling loudly."

Richard said he clambered back again, deciding that the best thing to do was to wait for me. When he got to the ledge, the man had gone! There was no sign that anyone had been there. Richard confessed he hadn't gone into the cave-mouth, beyond the ledge, and he didn't have to tell us why . . . he was frightened—frightened of injured and unconscious climbers who, once his back was turned, came to and walked away! He had climbed, himself, as fast as he could, up to the top of the cliff . . .

That was his story and I found it difficult to believe.

He saw the way I stared at him and, "I wondered if—if we had *imagined* it?" he faltered.

"*Of course,* we didn't imagine it!" I said, furiously. "I remember what he looked like. Fairhaired, with a blue shirt and grey flannels. I even remember he wore a ring on the little finger of his left hand. Men so seldom wear rings and when they do, it sticks in your mind. *Of course* we saw him!"

I don't know if Jed thought I was on the point

of climbing down again to see if the man had returned by this time, for, "Easy," he said, and held my arm. Slowly and deliberately, he went himself down the cliff-face. Neither of us followed. Richard sat, still pale, but having no more to say. His face plainly said, "That's my story and that's what happened. If you find it difficult to believe, I can't help that."

"It's very strange," I said, reluctantly, and that seemed an understatement.

Then Jed's head and shoulders appeared above the top of the cliffs and he pulled himself over. There was no expression on his face to indicate whether he was surprised or not—but then, I had never seen Jed look anything save what Sally called sad-and-sorry. He looked that way now, as he said, "No one there. I went a little way into the caves. No one there." He didn't say, "You imagined it," and I don't think he thought this. He did say, "Strange things happen on the cliffs," and seemed satisfied.

"That's not strange," I said. "It's impossible. He couldn't get up and walk away——"

"Maybe he was fetched?" Jed suggested but didn't enlarge on this. I shivered, suddenly. He looked at me and said, "Come along home. And don't tell Mrs. Letty."

We promised we wouldn't. "What is there to

tell?" I said. "How can we say we found a man, then lost him again?"

"That's right," Jed nodded, and took us back to the farm in the car.

If she noticed that we were quiet over tea, Mrs. Letty said nothing, but kept urging us to take "a little more of this" and "a slice of that." She and Jed saw us off at the bus stop. We were loaded, as always after a visit to the farm, with eggs and fruit. As we got into the bus, Jed leaned towards us and whispered, "Don't worry. Forget it."

We nodded. Mrs. Letty said, "What's that you said?" but Jed just shook his head, so she didn't question him.

I decided, on the way home in the bus, to do just that . . . forget it.

I didn't want any more mysteries—The Silver Circle—the Browns and Peter Blake—the disappearance of the ring—were more than enough. People who lay injured on cliffs, needing help, then disappearing—this was too much, and I told myself it had nothing to do with me. (I had no idea, when I thought this, how closely they were all bound up together, the mysteries that plagued and puzzled me, and how, though I had been miles away from the woods that afternoon, I had stumbled on yet another piece of the jigsaw to be slipped into place.)

We walked slowly from the bus to the house, loaded with parcels like pack-horses. Martha waited for us at the gate and helped us carry them in. I thought it strange she didn't ask how Mrs. Letty was and if there was a message from her. There was a message, and I delivered it, but Martha only nodded and slipped it into her pocket. I wondered what had gone wrong here in the house, and was on the point of asking, when Richard said, "Is Sally back yet?"

Martha looked grim. I said quickly, "Where *is* Sally, Martha? What's happened?"

She only said, "Go up to her, Livvy."

I went upstairs two at a time. Was Sally sick? I pushed open the bedroom door. I could hear her crying, the tired, hiccupping sob you give when you have cried so much, you haven't the strength to bawl—but you still can't stop, you feel so bad. For Sally, usually so calm and unruffled, to act this way, something must indeed be wrong! I couldn't think what it might be. I went over and shook her shoulder. "What is it? Sally, what happened?"

Richard stood in the doorway, as worried as I, looking awkward and inadequate, the way boys do, when there are tears. I remember thinking, "Poor Richard, he *has* had a bad day!"

"*What is it?*" I asked again. "Sally, tell us." Hoping to bring her back to normal, I said, "Did you finish the sketch?"

At that, she cried harder than ever. Richard and I looked at each other in alarm. Sally pointed to the portfolio she carried with her whenever she went sketching. I was always impressed by it and by the way it made her look important, like a real, grown-up artist, when she tucked it under her arm. Now I hesitated to open it, wondering what I should find.

But, "Open it," Richard whispered. I did, and could hardly believe my eyes at what I saw. The sketch of The Silver Circle over which Sally had worked so hard and which I was certain was the best thing she had ever done was scribbled over with thick charcoal—over and over, criss-crossed, this way and that, senselessly, like a baby's scribblings.

Sally's sketch was quite ruined now, and would never win a prize . . .

CHAPTER SIX

PETER BLAKE DISAPPEARS

RICHARD and I stood there, saying nothing, looking from the sketch to Sally. Neither of us wanted to say, "Don't cry," because we thought, as she did, it was a terrible thing to happen!

Then, "Do you want any supper?" Richard whispered. It was probably the most comforting thing he could think of.

Sally shook her head but Martha, appearing in the doorway, said, "Oh yes, she does," and came in with a tray on which was a glass of milk and some biscuits. "You go down," she told us, and we went. Later, we sat one on each side of the supper table, Martha between us, but it was a silent meal, and we were glad to say good-night and go quietly upstairs. Richard crept behind me, into our room. Sally was sitting up in bed, her eyes red and swollen, but at least she had stopped crying. We stood in front of her, like a couple of owls, and waited for her to tell us what had happened.

She couldn't speak of it, even now, without tears coming, but we did manage to get the story from her. She had finished earlier than she thought

because her sketch didn't need many "touches".
She didn't want to come back to the house, since
Richard and I were not there, so she decided to go
along and see Kim. Sally hadn't yet seen Kim's
sketch, nor Kim Sally's, and each was curious about
the other.

(When she said this, my eyes flew to the portfolio
in which lay the ruined sketch. A crazy thought
came into my mind, so crazy and utterly impossible
that I reddened, there in front of the others. Of
course, nothing like *that* had happened . . .)

"I went along and Kim showed me her sketch of
The White Veil. It's good," Sally said, in a low
voice. "It will take a prize." We waited uncomfortably while she wiped away more tears.

"Yours will win, too," Richard said, unthink-
ingly. "I mean," he floundered and I said,
"S-sh," impatiently, not wanting him to make
matters worse.

They had both praised each other's work. "We
talked about all kinds of things. We shared our
tea." Sally kept stopping so that you had to prompt
her to go on.

I heaved a sigh of relief. Then, however the accident had happened to Sally's sketch, it couldn't
have been Kim. I said, aloud, "It had nothing to
do with Kim, then?"

Sally didn't answer.

Richard said, "But when did you find it—like that?" He jerked his head towards the sketch.

"When I came home, Martha asked to see it. I opened the portfolio, and that's the way it was."

"You had the portfolio with you, all the time, didn't you?" I asked. "When you were with Kim, you took it with you—you didn't leave it, anywhere?"

"I took it with me," she said, "but I left it with Kim when I went down the bank."

It took me some time to realise exactly what she had said. When I did, I could only say, weakly, "Why did you go down the bank?"

"Kim had been telling me *you* took her to the cave beneath the fall. I remembered I hadn't been there for years, and I wanted to see it again. I asked her if she would come but she said no—she wanted to finish her painting. I didn't get to the bottom of the bank. There was a puppy, half-way down. He belongs to the people who live in that white house, close to the fall. He was scared about climbing up again, so I had to chase him and carry him."

"How long did this take?" Richard asked.

"Not more than ten minutes."

(*Ten minutes!* Long enough for someone to open the portfolio, scribble on the sketch, put it back—so making sure one competitor with a good chance of winning was out of the running. I told myself to stop thinking this but sometimes thoughts you don't want keep coming into your head and won't leave.)

"You are certain you didn't leave it anywhere else?" I almost pleaded.

"I took it into the inn with me, but there was no one there. I went through all the rooms. I had time and there was no danger, in daylight. I left it on the window-seat, in the room nearest the door," Sally said, "but there was *no one* at the inn. It was empty."

"It couldn't be Kim," I said, putting into words what we all thought. "You *know* that's impossible——"

Neither of them spoke.

I lay awake, long after Sally slept. It had been a day of mysteries, I thought, but what had happened to Sally put everything else out of my mind. I knew she was terribly disappointed—we all were —but, at the same time, in spite of the way the evidence looked, I would not for a moment believe Kim had done such a mean and despicable trick. But who else? There I was stuck for an answer. No one who was going in for the Competition had been where Sally was that afternoon—save Kim.

Mummy came home next day, and her first question was, "Sally, where is the sketch? It must be finished—let me see it." When Sally told her what had happened, Mummy was as upset as anyone. She looked at the ruined sketch, with the senseless charcoal scribblings, and had nothing to say. It was

the same with us all—no one could give an explanation—but we each echoed Martha, when she muttered, "If I could get my hands on the one who did
it . . ."

It was too late for Sally to attempt anything else,
even if she had the heart to do this, and I believed
her when she said she didn't want to see her sketch-
book or The Silver Circle again for a long time! It
was a terrible shame to think of all the work and the
hours she had put into her sketching gone for
nothing!

Although she had just come home, Mummy took
Sally away for the day to visit cousins, hoping it
would help her to forget. Richard went off to see a
County cricket match so I was left alone. I played
with Emma and Noel all morning, but in the after-
noon Martha took them to a children's party. When
I went up to my room, I found a note there from
Richard.

*Forgot to ask you—will you return this book to
P. Blake for me. Thanks, Richard. P.S.—If you
feel too scared to go, don't.*

That was clever of him, I thought, grimly! Now,
of course, there was nothing for me to do but go.
Anyway, I thought, the caravan was some distance
away from The Silver Circle and I needn't go near
the inn, if I didn't want to! (I think, from every-

thing that had happened there, I had almost come to believe it had hypnotic qualities and could force you towards it . . .) Also, I could simply return Richard's book to "P. Blake", bid him a polite good-afternoon, and leave.

It didn't turn out like that at all.

I have always loved caravans. I envy the people who come to Fold in the summer, and camp outside the town, living in their caravans, bathing almost from their doorsteps. I tell myself I should dearly like a gypsy life, roaming the byways, camping when and where I felt inclined—beyond that hill— beside this river—moving on when one place failed to attract. Sally throws cold water on my dreams by telling me I should need towns and shops and so on. "After all, you weren't born and brought up a gypsy," she argues. "You have to be—to enjoy it." Perhaps she is right and a caravan is at its best only a holiday home—but I certainly envied Peter Blake his.

He was there when I arrived, but the grass was soft and he didn't hear me. I had time to study him. He certainly didn't look like anyone's idea of a criminal. He was fair-haired and slight, with a face which lit up with a smile that told you he was really glad to see you. It seemed a pity, I decided, that all that had happened in South America, for it never occurred to me to doubt Mary Brown's story. It was a pity he couldn't forget about it and start afresh. I wondered if he were thinking of it now, as he sat there, staring into space.

He rose as I came in sight. "Ah—the Head of the Family! Neither the artist nor the engineer. What is it to be, Livvy?"

There and then, I forgot I had meant to say, "Here is the book you lent Richard. Thank you. Good-bye." I sat next to him, quite happily, and said I hadn't decided yet.

"Don't let it worry you," he said comfortingly. "You'll know, when the time comes." He seemed glad of company and was so kind and so amusing that I pushed Mary's story to the back of my mind, and prepared to enjoy the afternoon. We talked of caravans and he said he loved the life too. I asked him if shops and towns made all that difference— and he said no, not if you stocked up at the last shop or town. He said he couldn't indulge in it as often as he would like, but there was one trip he had made —to Spain.

I sat there, listening without interruption, while he told me of the trip to Spain—mountains and sun —grapes and old cities!

"You do get around!" I marvelled. "Spain— Australia—Sweden——"

As I said this, I remembered it had been *Mary* who had told me he had followed them to Sweden, and I could have bitten back the words! I didn't want to give her away but perhaps he hadn't noticed for he went on talking. Then I asked if he had handed in his painting for the Competition. "To-day is the day. You have to take it to the Town Hall." Privately, I didn't think it stood much chance but if he were really fond of painting, it wasn't up to me to spoil his fun.

He paused. He looked at me. *"No,"* he said. "I'm not taking it."

"Why not? After all, you've spent some time on it." Now he was obviously reluctant, I tried to persuade him to send it in. He seemed to be weighing me up, deciding whether he should tell me more, and I must have seemed truthworthy for he rose and went up the steps of the caravan. I waited. I knew there was more to the story. He came back, carrying a canvas. When he turned it round, I saw that the picture of the inn as he had painted it was slashed across and completely ruined.

I had the same feeling of horror and disbelief as when Sally had shown me her ruined drawing. When I could speak, "That makes two," I croaked.

"Two?" The way he snapped out the word made me jump.

I told him what had happened to Sally's sketch.

When he heard what I had to say, he smiled—nothing horrid or spiteful—but a smile as though he were saying to himself, *"Of course,"* and he gave a satisfied little sigh.

But nothing made sense to me, and I shook my

head as I stared at the painting. "There must be people who are determined not to have The Silver Circle publicised," I said.

"Indeed, you are right," he murmured, half to himself. Then, "Poor Sally—is she much upset?"

"Yes," I said. "Are you?"

He shook his head. "It wasn't a very good painting."

"It didn't deserve to be slashed," I told him firmly.

He laughed aloud.

Then he asked me if I would care to stay to tea, and I said yes—if I could *make tea*. I thought it would be a fine opportunity for poking round the caravan and getting to know the lay of it. Best of all, I loved the tiny stove and the small pots of geraniums he had growing. I tested the bed and found it comfortable—and I fiddled with the table until I knew exactly how it let down from the wall. I longed to ask how much such a caravan cost and decided I would, when I knew him better, so that I could start saving in earnest.

I opened all the cupboards and doors I saw but he didn't seem to mind. I read the titles on the row of books (they were mostly on cricket) and I had completely forgotten what it was I had heard of him. To me, at the moment, he was a friend who was amiably providing me with a very pleasant afternoon.

Then something happened that brought it all back.

One drawer stuck, as I pulled at it. He had told me the cutlery was kept in it, and I wanted tea-spoons and knives, since I was determined to have everything in order for this first caravan-meal I had prepared! I pulled—but, as is the contrary way of drawers, when I gave a sharp tug, it come out quickly and unexpectedly. "I *am* sorry," I called. He was still sitting outside, to give me more room to move about the caravan, and I heard him say it was all right. I stooped to pick up the things that had fallen on to the floor. As I bent down, my eye caught the glitter of something bright. I looked closer. Rolling on the floor of the caravan, from where it had lain hidden at the back of the drawer, was a silver ring—and I was *certain* it was the one Sally had found and lost again. So it *was* Peter Blake, I told myself, who had pumped the story from Richard, climbed up on to our veranda, into the bedroom, and searched there until he found, in our innocent-looking chocolate-box, what he had been seeking . . .

Carefully, I put the ring back into the drawer. I found spoons and knives. I made the tea and took it out to him on the tray. For him, nothing seemed to have changed, for, as easily and pleasantly as before, he offered me a chocolate biscuit. I hoped *I* looked and sounded as though nothing had happened! From now on, he did most of the talking and, if he noticed my flow of talk had dried up, he said nothing but went on being pleasant. I helped to wash up afterwards. I said good-bye, and thanked him for the book he insisted I took back to Richard, in exchange for the one I had brought. "When do you want it back?" I asked. He said any time—he wouldn't be leaving the place in a hurry.

"If you do want it back quickly," I said, not thinking what I was saying, "you know where we live?"

"Yes. I know where your home is. The veranda with the pillars——" He stopped smiling and said, surprised, "What's the matter, Livvy? What have I said?"

"Nothing," I choked. "Good-afternoon."

I thought, as I left, that he certainly was afraid of very little! If he had climbed into Sally's room to search for the ring, he certainly thought little of it, to joke so easily and flippantly . . .

All the way back to Fold, I was furious that, for all my good intentions, I had landed myself, by the simple task of making tea for Peter Blake, plumb into the middle of another clue—and this time, one so easy and so obvious, it didn't need much thinking out.

Mystery grew on mystery, I told myself, like a tree growing and putting out branches and leaves.

Yet, all the time, I had the feeling these were only lesser mysteries—rings and footsteps, even spoiled drawings—in themselves, they might loom large in our minds, but I was sure they only pointed the way to something bigger than anything we could imagine. I didn't know if the others thought the way I did—perhaps not, because they didn't know as much about Peter Blake, for instance. But before he had come along—the first time we had become involved with The Silver Circle—that feeling had stayed with me, that it was the centre of something too big for us to comprehend, something it would be better, for our sakes, to leave alone.

I walked along, thinking of all that had happened —trying, once more, to piece it together and to make sense. Why, I asked myself—because my thoughts were centred on the ring I had found in the caravan —did I immediately think of the man Richard and I had found on the cliff? *Why?* There must be some connection and it nagged at me. I felt cross and bad-tempered and, I confess, more than a little scared. It seemed as though we got deeper into the maze every day.

"Livvy," a voice said, and I looked up. I was walking along the Front at Fold, deep in my thoughts. I may have passed many of my friends, without seeing them, or without hearing if they had called me. But Mary Brown took hold of my arm and made me come back to earth again. I remem-

bered, as I smiled at her, that we didn't see much
of her these days. Then, I remembered that was
because she preferred to keep out of the way of
Peter Blake—and there I was again!

"What's the matter, Livvy? Something must be
wrong to make you scowl this way?"

I gave the stock answer, *"Nothing."* But,
"Nonsense!" Mary said. "There is something
wrong and I insist you tell me so that I can try to
help. But first, let's go in here," and she led the way
into Fold's largest and shiniest café, a place we
three young Taylors frequented rarely, since it was
'way beyond our means. I wished I had on a clean
frock or had tidied my hair. Mary must have known
how I felt for she said, "Don't worry. What will
you have?" Then she ordered what she had known
I wanted but didn't like to ask for—the biggest nut
sundae they made. "Where have you been?" she
asked. I told her and her face darkened. I hated
myself for reminding her of Peter Blake, just then,
when she seemed happy and carefree. But she said,
"What happened, there? You enjoyed your visit?
He can be very charming, I know."

"I enjoyed it until——" I paused.

"Until what, Livvy?"

"Until I found the ring," I said.

"What ring?"

So I told her everything—about Sally finding the
silver ring and putting it safely away—about the

burglary and how everything pointed to Peter Blake having done it—and about the second (or the same) ring I had found, in his caravan, that afternoon. I told her about the stranger on the cliffs. I left nothing out and she listened intently to every word. It always helps to tell someone what it is that worries you, and I thought it very good of Mary to listen, the way she did. After all, I knew she had troubles that worried her too. Hadn't she confided, a little, in me? I had almost finished my second sundae when I stopped and said, "That's all."

She smiled. "Isn't it enough, Livvy?" She paused and put her hand over mine and held it tight.

"Yes," I said. I must have looked particularly serious for she said, as if to herself, "I wonder if it's fair to tell you?"

"Whatever it is, it's worse *not* to tell me," I said, bluntly, "now you've started!"

"I suppose so. All right, then." She drew a deep breath and so did I. "It is serious. Livvy—more serious than you think. What I told you about Blake . . . you remember?" I nodded. "That was just a personal aspect of the matter," she said. "It goes much further and it is strange my brother Hugh should be connected with both stories. Strange— and poetic justice."

I wasn't sure what particular kind of justice that was but I went on spooning up the last of the ice-cream, listening to her as she had listened to me. One thing, though, I didn't want to look at her. While I listened to the words, I could almost pretend it was a story about someone else—some people we didn't know and who were in no way connected with us—so I stared at my milky glass dish.

"It was clever of Sally to think there might be a connection between the ring and the inn—the two 'silver circles.' There is an organisation operating under that name. So her guess—her intuition—was right." She was silent for a while, then said again, in a worried tone, "Livvy, I *can* trust you?"

I nodded. I couldn't say anything. I remembered the keen look Peter Blake had given me, as though asking the same question, before he showed me his ruined painting. I could almost wish I didn't appear so very trustworthy. My heart was knocking so hard, I was surprised she didn't hear it and comment.

"I'll tell you, then. I really did play with the idea of buying the inn. It is true that I am looking for a place in the country, hidden away from everywhere. I am beginning to think I have had more than my share of travel and excitement. I want to settle down, now, in a country home—dogs, a large garden . . . Anyway," she went on, quickly, "I want you to know I did think The Silver Circle an ideal place, when I told you about it, the first day we met. But Hugh was there for another reason. He is working with the authorities."

I looked up then, and found her gazing searchingly at me.

"Surprised? You'll understand I can't go into details but I must give you a vague outline and satisfy a little of what you must be wondering. We didn't want to frighten you away—and Sally's sketch was so important."

I remembered I hadn't told her what had happened to *that*—time enough, I thought. I had as much as I could do, taking in what Mary was saying. She went on, "When I saw Blake that day, my fears were confirmed. If he is mixed up in what Hugh is trying to track down, it is just what he would do. The other matter between us frightened me too, for as I told you, he would not let himself forget. Anyway, the inn is the centre of most of what is happening and I hope"—she looked hard at me—"you will keep away, from now on. It isn't safe. I'm telling you this for your own good. I don't want any harm to come to you."

"The police know, of course?" I managed to say.

She didn't answer directly but said, "I have trusted you with a big secret, Livvy. I don't have to tell you not to tell anyone. I think I've judged you aright. Sally is too wrapped up in her drawing. Richard, as any boy would be, is pro-Blake for, as

I've said, he has a certain charm. But I've judged *you* as the steadiest of the three.''

I didn't know about that. At times, I felt far from steady—as when I heard those footsteps at the inn—still, it was a compliment and I tried to look as if I had earned it.

Mary went on, ''That man you found on the cliff?''

''Richard says we may have dreamed him up.''

''Of course you didn't! You say you believe there was a link between him and what has been happening at the inn? *Why* should you think that? There must be a reason. The spot is some distance from the woods—on the other side of Fold. *What* makes you link them together? *Think*, Livvy—it may help us more than you know! I may as well tell you—time is running short and we have to act quickly. *Why* did you think he might have something to do with The Silver Circle?''

I did as she said. I thought hard. Then—''The ring!'' I said. ''He had a ring on his left little finger. It was a ring like the one Sally found. I remember looking at it because it isn't often you see men wearing rings.''

She was silent, for a time, thinking deeply. Then she squeezed my hand, again, hard. ''Livvy, you really have helped.''

I didn't know in what way, but if what I had remembered was part of a vital clue, I was glad to have supplied it. My mind, by this time, was a whirl of rings and secrets and inns and people pretending to be what they were not. "I'm going to ask you to help some more, now you know so much," Mary said, and I felt one with the C.I.D. There *must* be some strain of sleuthing, far back in our family. It has come out strongly in Richard, and was now faintly stirring in me. I said, "*Yes?*" eagerly and quickly, as though awaiting vital and secret orders.

"If you see Blake do anything suspicious—anything you think we should know—will you come straight to me? I don't mean," Mary said, "that you should *trail* him. Nothing so melodramatic and I don't want to expose you to danger. But he won't suspect *you* of helping *us*—and it will help, Livvy, I assure you."

Perhaps it was the way she stressed the word *help*—but I promised. She was looking squarely and appealingly at me and I felt I would—and could —do anything to help her.

We left the café then, and went our separate ways. If I was quiet that evening, and had little to say, it was overlooked by the family. Deep down inside, in spite of Mary's assurances about not wanting me to be in any danger, I admit I felt a little scared when I thought of what was going on —and I knew Daddy and Mummy would be very angry if they knew how deeply I was involved. I couldn't tell them, of course, for I had given a pro-

mise to keep everything secret. When it was over
and the case solved and everyone knew all about it,
perhaps, I told myself, I might confess to my part
. . . even then, I wasn't sure!

Sally, we considered, was being wonderfully
brave and grown-up about the loss of her sketch
and everyone tried, in all sorts of ways, to show how
they sympathised with her. Next year, I thought,
she can try again. But next year, I was certain her
subject wouldn't be The Silver Circle!

She wouldn't come near the woods any more.
True to my promise to Mary Brown, I decided I
would go to see Peter Blake next day, to see what
he was doing and to make up my mind whether or
not it seemed suspicious. Richard and I went
together and I remember thinking what a pity it was
he and I couldn't change places. *He* would have
loved to act sleuth, though not, perhaps, to Peter
Blake!

When we got to where the caravan had been
parked, there was no one there! "He can't have
gone without saying good-bye?" Richard said, disappointedly.

I looked round. There was no sign, no clue.
"But only yesterday he told me he wouldn't leave
here in a hurry. *You* could bring the book back
any time," I protested.

"He must have been called away suddenly,"
Richard said.

"*Why?*" I asked, sounding nasty. "He doesn't *do* anything—no job, I mean."

Richard demanded how I knew this. Mr. Blake was on holiday and it had come to an end—why must I always be so suspicious about him? Even if I didn't like him, I was making myself ridiculous —so Richard went on, defending Peter Blake, though I knew most of it was disappointment that he had left without a word.

I wanted to say, "Oh, Richard, stop! If you only knew what I know . . ." But I had to keep silent.

We made one or two casual inquiries but no one knew where the caravan had gone. Peter Blake was a stranger to Fold and there were thousands of strangers who came and went, in the summer season, and more than one green and cream caravan.

It was an unexpected development and I did not know what to make of it but when I said this to Mary, she murmured, "He will come back. I told you time was running short and this proves it. But we haven't seen the last of him, Livvy. Don't think that. He'll turn up again, and at The Silver Circle!"

CHAPTER SEVEN

THE CLUE IN THE WOOD

THE next day saw the beginning of Carnival Week in Fold and, entering into the spirit of it, I was glad to forget the secrets and suspicions that worried and bewildered me. I was scared in case I made some slip and Sally and Richard (who can be *very* quick off the mark, when they wish!) were on to what I knew and was hiding—and had ferreted Mary Brown's story out of me.

When I knew Peter Blake had disappeared, I did not go near the woods, glad of a reason to keep away.

Anyway, now that the Carnival was here, I had no thoughts for anything else. We roamed the streets, admiring the way they were decorated with flags and bunting. We went to the sports meetings and exhibitions. We watched the yacht race. We did all the things everyone did—and which we had done, every year, but which never failed to thrill us.

The great event of the week was the Carnival Fancy-Dress Parade, and Mummy let us enter every year. Our friends did the same—and there were just two reasons why you were excused fancy dress, on this particular afternoon—either you were in bed too ill to walk—or you were away from Fold altogether!

We always hoped for a fine day—though, of course, we had our share of dull and rainy weather —but when the sun shone and the sea glittered and the flags dipped and waved, Fold really was in carnival mood, like those continental cities which enter so easily into the holiday spirit—through having so much sun for so long a time, I suppose. Hundreds of people came in to see the procession. There was a band in front and a visiting band at the rear. (They had been known to play different tunes at the same time!) Everywhere, in every street and square, was colour and laughter and excitement. It really was like France or Italy or Spain, I imagined—because we English don't often or easily *let ourselves go,* do we? (Maybe that is on account of the weather too!)

We kept our fingers crossed for a fine day this year, and it was perfect, with a haze in the morning out to sea which promised glorious sunshine. The glass was going up—all the signs were promising— and there was nothing to worry about. I had tried to persuade Kim to join our Parade but she said she would prefer to watch, this first time. If she walked in the Parade, she could see only *part* of everything.

"Next year," she promised, "we'll go into the Parade together, Livvy."

"You are coming back, then, next year?" I asked. "Kim, that will be grand!"

She told me she meant to spend most of the school holidays from now on at Fold. I didn't know whether that was because of *us*, or her grandfather, but preferred to think it might be because of both!

But Sally never came with me now, when I went to meet Kim. I don't know if Kim guessed what Sally thought. I said nothing at all to Kim about the ruined sketch and she, too, never spoke of it but the thought of what had happened hung like a shadow over the three of us. *I* couldn't find any explanation, try as I might. I did tell Sally, when I described to her how I had been shown Peter Blake's ruined picture, too, "You know *Kim* couldn't have done that—even if you think she may have spoiled yours—and you *can't* think she did!"

"I don't know what to think and I don't want to think!" my sister said forcefully. "All I know is a lot of work went for nothing and I'm sick of mystery. I never care if I see The Silver Circle again!"

That was that—and I agreed with her. I did not remind her it was *she* who had been anxious to go there in the first place.

Sally, with her long fair plaits, went to the Carnival as Maid Marian. She looked well in her green costume, and a friend of ours, Larry Miles, went with her as Robin Hood. They had decided to enter the section for competitors who went in *pairs* but they ended under the heading of *groups*. For when one of the other boys, in our road, wanted to go as Friar Tuck, and another as Little John, the idea grew until they had the whole Robin Hood band! I thought it a wonderful idea, and told Sally that of course they would get a prize. "If we do," she said, thoughtfully, "it will have to be divided between *seven*." I told her not to be mercenary. Where was her usual answer of Art for Art's sake? This really did silence her—and I felt pleased with myself!

Richard and I wore the Tyrolean costumes an aunt had brought back last year. "Wear them," Martha advised, "because they'll soon be too small." I think she would have considered it more suitable if Aunt Bet had brought back a dress length for me or a shirt for Richard but Aunt Bet had chosen these gay national costumes, and though I suppose they were impractical and we would never "wear them out", I loved them for their brightness and gaiety and the pretty embroidery. Richard wasn't so enthusiastic but at least I think he considered them easier to wear than some of the costumes we had seen in the past. I loved the short, full skirt and crisp white blouse and embroidered bodice. When I was dressed and went to show Martha the way I looked, she unbent enough to say we *might* get a prize—"if we didn't go and spoil things by doing something silly"—though, when she said it, she didn't know *I* should be the one who would go and do just this! She was thinking of Richard.

The Parade was due to start at two o'clock but, as always happened, it was still forming at two-thirty! Once it got started, it was as much fun as ever because, while you paraded to the rousing music, you could never feel you were the ordinary day-to-day person who lived and went to school in Fold! You might imagine you were living, for a few hours, in the pages of a book whose characters had come to life around you! It was a time when *anything* might happen and, when it did, it would be magical and exciting. There was the surprise of meeting and recognising (and not recognising) friends in their fancy dress. We *always* said, "*Fancy* so-and-so coming *as that*!" or "That costume looks *just right* on so-and-so!" Most probably, they criticised us that way!

I could never walk properly for laughing at the men on stilts with fantastic heads which ducked and bobbed and leered at the crowd! Then I had to turn, from time to time, to look at the floats which were crawling along behind us. The Mayor was there, in his scarlet (*not t*o be confused with fancy dress!)—the sea and sky were blue—the sand golden—and the streets of the town sparkled in the sunshine. It was a day to remember all the year round, particularly on the grey, miserable, rainy days which, of course, would come—even in Fold!

We walked through the town, then along the Front, to be judged finally on the Pier. Richard walked on one side of me, and on the other was a black cat who obviously belonged to Dick Whittington walking along on his right. Dick looked cool and elegant in tights and a jerkin and a hat with a feather. But it was a hot day and the cat, in black velvet, with mask and gummed whiskers, was inclined to droop. He agreed it would have been cooler at Highgate, listening to the bells of London!

When we reached the Pier, the gates were opened and we all marched on to it, for it was cleared of visitors for the day, and the Carnival Committee waited there, and the Mayor, to judge and present prizes. The floats couldn't come on to the Pier so they turned up the street leading to the Castle and were judged there. People who wanted to watch the judging of *everything* were torn between the Pier and the Castle and usually had to make dashes from one to the other.

The prizes which were given were always very good and those who won them were pleased and proud—and with the pictures that went into the newspaper. In the evening we had fireworks and a beacon lit on the hill and coloured lights everywhere —and usually, we went to bed on Carnival night, sorry that it was over but certain that we couldn't have faced another such day for at least a year!

Dick and his cat stood farther up the line, waiting to be judged, and we had next to us an Orange and a Lemon. Before he wore the fancy dress, the Orange must have been a short, tubby boy. Now, in his round orange dress over wooden supports, he looked just like a ball. Like the cat, he wasn't too happy about it and I took the opportunity to tell Richard how pleased *he* should be that *we* had decided on something as sensible as the Tyrolean costumes!

The Committee judged thoroughly—no skimping —so that it took a long time. They went, in a group, from one to another and back again, laughing, pointing, smiling, frowning—not with annoyance but with concentration. I knew most of them but, of course, they would frown on me as hard as at any stranger. At least, they would have done, if they had come anywhere near judging me. You see, I *didn't wait to be judged*! As Richard wrathfully said, afterwards, I took the trouble to dress up, walk round the town, march on to the Pier and stand there until the judges were within half-a-dozen people of me—then I ran off as fast as I could! I know that was the way it appeared to him and to anyone else who saw me go—but that was after I had seen the tramp!

For a time, when you are in a colourful, mixed-

up throng like this, you can't take in all the costumes. They appear a jumble, like a kaleidoscope.
Then, as time passes, you pick out one or another.
You see a face you know—a costume illustrating a
book or rhyme you recognise—someone looks so
realistic, you spend some time over him—like the
shockingly disreputable old tramp, at the end of the
line, opposite me. In this gathering of gay, bright,
clean colours, he stood out, startlingly, as a
chimney-sweep might at a garden party! His hat
was broken, his shoes held together by string, there
were rents and holes in his sleeves—his suit was
what no respectable scarecrow would own—but, in
spite of all this, there was something *familiar* about
him!

I told myself not to be silly. I didn't know any
tramps—not to recognise again. When I did meet
one, I was careful to put as much distance between
us as possible. But this tramp, outwardly dirtier
and poorer than any I had seen, was definitely
familiar. I stared harder. He saw me do this, looked
at me, once, then quickly turned away so that the
brim of that awful hat hid his face from me. He
looked as if he recognised me too, at that instant,
for he looked the way you do when you see someone
you know but don't wish to speak to—when you
hope they won't recognise you.

I nudged Richard. He was deep in conversation
with the Orange whose face, by this time, was some

degrees darker than his "skin". "Richard," I
said, "The tramp, over there—who does he remind
you of?"

The Orange looked, too. "Golly," he said,
"what a good disguise! I wish I'd thought of it.
Sensible, too! You don't have to be careful, in those
clothes. You can just forget about them——"

I wasn't listening to the Orange though I told myself that next year it would be certain *he* would
come as a *tramp*! "Richard!" I persisted.

"*It's Peter Blake!*"

I nodded. I wasn't interested in what Richard
might say next. The Orange's word—*disguise*—
had been enough. I could see the bitter look on
Mary Brown's face when she told me her story—
and the intent look, when she asked me to help her.
I could hear myself promising to tell her, at once,
if Peter Blake did anything I thought was suspicious. *This,* I told myself, was suspicious—to disappear without a trace from the woods, and reap-
pear here, disguised as a tramp. He was probably
using the Carnival and fancy dress as an excuse for
slipping back into town, without being recognised
by anyone who might have known him as the owner
of the caravan in the woods, the painter of indif-
ferent pictures. Anyone, dressed as a tramp, could
wander the countryside in summer without rousing
over-much suspicion. Where was it he wanted to
go—and why? Who was it he wished to trail?

As I was thinking this, he moved from his place in the line, swiftly, easily, so as to draw no attention to himself, though he wouldn't have been commented on in that crowd, for it was a day when most people did as they pleased and went where they wished. Once on the streets, he would be quite safe, for no one would think the "tramp" had ever entered the Carnival procession. People did question him as he made for the gates of the Pier. Perhaps they asked him why he wasn't waiting for the Mayor and the judges. His answer must have satisfied them, for I watched them smile and, in a minute, he was lost from sight.

I didn't know what to do. I was enjoying the Parade, as much as I always did. It was the day of the year for us, and I didn't want to leave it. We might get a prize, Richard and I, with our Tyrolean costumes. (Though I thought the depressed-looking Orange would benefit more from it!) Still, all these thoughts going through my mind didn't take very long. A minute after Peter Blake disappeared, I followed him.

Neither Sally nor Richard saw me go for they were facing the judges who were coming nearer, every minute, and were now only three places away. "I've spoiled my chance and Richard's," I thought.

Some people called to me, "Wait a minute!" "Won't be long, now!" but I didn't smile and murmur an excuse, the way Peter Blake might have done. I kept on, grimly threading my way between them, until I was at the entrance to the Pier and on the Promenade. I forgot everything in my anxiety to keep the "tramp" in sight. If he had a car waiting, of course, that would put an end to my plans, but luckily, wherever he was going, it was to be on foot. I saw him turn up Castle Street. It was easy to keep sight of him in those shocking clothes because I don't think he could hurry with his shoes flapping and tied with string. *I* looked far more conspicuous now than he, in my dress which would have been in place only in the Austrian Tyrol! But to-day, Fold was in carnival mood, and apart from one or two smiles and pointing fingers, I managed to pass without meeting a friend or acquaintance who would say, "Livvy, aren't you in the wrong part of the town?"

Of course, I told myself sourly, as I had when I first recognised him, the point of the "tramp" costume was that he could slip by, unnoticed. I didn't, for one moment, believe Peter Blake had intended going to the Fancy Dress Carnival, like the others of us, for fun or for a prize. He had meant people to think he had left the district for good. Someone might recognise him, if he came back, and obviously he didn't want that. As a tramp, he could slip into the woods, unnoticed and without arousing comment. Tramps seemed to favour Farley Woods, in summer, and one more could walk there, and make it his home.

We climbed up, away from the beach, through the cobbled streets, choosing those where the shops were mostly closed and their owners gone to watch the Carnival. We went past the Castle but on the side where there was no crowd. Then we crossed the river and began making our way towards the woods. It was a long walk and he walked quickly when we got to the grass, for he stooped, took off his shoes and threw them away. I couldn't throw mine away though I got hot and tired, but I grimly followed him. If he once looked back, I thought, when we were on the stretch of grass before he came to the shelter of the trees, I should be discovered and lost, for my costume, with its bright green and red and blue, showed up against grass and sky, shouting aloud to be noticed—telling him that I was all the time behind him, acting the part of sleuth. I didn't know clearly what I meant to do, at the end of this trailing of him, nor what was likely to come next. I did know that when I went back I would find Mary Brown and tell her what had happened. It was what she had asked me to do —and anyway, I was working on the side of authority, I told myself with what must have been smugness!

It was more difficult to keep him in sight between the trees. The dark, tattered figure seemed to slip between the trunks like a shadow. But I was *certain* I knew where he was going. From the beginning I had known and, if I lost sight of him, I would have gone to one place and been almost sure he was there—back to The Silver Circle where, it seemed, everything began and ended, and which was the centre of all these mysterious moves. I had thought this before, and had no reason to change my mind.

We passed the inn. I could see it, secret and withdrawn, through the trees. Then he turned to the right and hurried on, for nearly half a mile. I almost lost him there, and it was only by the sound of the twigs snapping in the undergrowth that I knew where he was. I saw him stop at last, and I hid behind a tree. He didn't waste any time. Immediately, he started digging. He must have carried something in his pocket to dig with, for he worked silently and fast.

I never took my eyes away from him but I couldn't see—for his back hid what he was doing—whether he found anything or was burying something. I waited and he worked. He was there for perhaps ten minutes, then, when he rose and turned towards me, I hid behind the undergrowth. He never saw me and this time, when he was out of sight, I didn't follow but stayed there, staring at the spot where he had been . . .

I had never meant to follow him back. I couldn't hope to keep track of him, all the time. I decided

I had done enough sleuthing, for one day. I was tired and still hot, and I decided to stay there, and think things over. It was no good going back to the Carnival. That was out of the question!

Also, *I* meant to dig in the ground, too! I wanted to see what it was he had hidden.

When I thought it was safe, and that there was no danger of him coming back, I rose and went across. I could see where the ground had been freshly turned over. Of course, in the midst of all the shrubs and young saplings, you wouldn't notice it, if you weren't looking for it, but I did what Peter Blake had done—scraped back the soil. He may have used a knife—I had only a stick—but it served my purpose.

To anyone coming upon me suddenly, I must have looked strange, grubbing there in my fanciful costume, lost to everything, because a voice, when it said, behind me, "What on earth are you doing?" nearly made me jump out of my skin, with fright.

I looked round.

"Richard . . .!"

I was so glad it wasn't Peter Blake that I welcomed Richard with more enthusiasm than usual. He didn't return it. He was red-faced, short of breath and short of temper. His hair stuck up, his eyes were fiery-bright, and he could hardly get the words out, for anger.

"I *knew* you would come here! You say you don't like the place—you won't have anything to do with it—yet, you can't keep away! What are you looking for? I was *certain* we should have got a prize—but we had to stay together! There's no prize for *half* a costume—so there wasn't any point in *me* staying!" Not that Richard cared all that much about the prize but he considered, reasonably, that if we had taken the trouble to dress up and walk in the procession through Fold, we might as well wait to be judged. "What are you doing, here, grubbing like that?" he demanded.

Before I told him, I had to say, "Richard, it *was* the Orange, wasn't it?"

"Yes," he said, shortly. "First prize—he and the Lemon. They jolly well deserved it, too! But it might have been us, if we had stayed there! What *are* you up to?" he repeated.

I wanted to tell him everything—all that Mary had told me and the promise I had made that, if Peter Blake did anything I thought suspicious, I would try to find out what I could, then tell her. But how could I say this when I had also promised Mary it should be a secret between her and me? It was very difficult and I found I had *nothing* to say. Richard, though, answered himself . . .

"You think Peter Blake is mixed up in something shady?" The way he said it showed his vast scorn of the idea. To him, it was as unlikely Blake should be a criminal as—as *Kim*, I suppose. "You think he took Sally's ring, don't you? You think there's something suspicious going on at The Silver Circle he is mixed up in—*don't you*?" he demanded.

I didn't say yes or no. There was so much to say—and I could say none of it—so I kept silent. He grew even more exasperated. "I never heard such rot."

"Why is it rot?" I asked, stung to self-defence. "Why should he come to the Carnival, dressed as a tramp? He didn't want to be one of the Carnival crowd. He didn't want to win a prize. The clothes he wore were not fancy dress. They were disguise—that was what the Orange said, as soon as he saw them! Why should he run away and come here and start digging in the ground? Normal, honest-to-goodness people don't do that. He *knew* everyone at Fold would be watching the Procession to-day, and if anyone did see him, they would think him a tramp. It isn't what an ordinary person would do, *is it*? Just because he plays cricket——"

We were in for a first-class row. Then Richard muttered, as if he couldn't help it, "What *is* in the ground?" He said it reluctantly but he was plainly curious.

"I don't know," I said, shortly. "Why don't you help me find out?"

He hesitated, then began digging. I know he was torn between curiosity and a belief that there *was* something strange in Peter Blake's actions this afternoon, and his liking for the man. We dug in silence until my fingers found something soft and silky. I pulled it out.

"Parachute silk," Richard breathed. He looked at me in silence, and I stared back, puzzled. I didn't know what to say and had no explanation to give. I didn't know what I had expected to find, so carefully hidden—money, I suppose. Certainly not this soft piece of silk. I remembered stories I had heard of airmen baling out in enemy territory who had buried their parachutes so that no one should find them—but how did that link up with Peter Blake and The Silver Circle. You couldn't parachute down in to the woods without running grave risk of being caught on a branch . . . but *who* was parachuting? And why? And *from where*?

Richard pulled it out, shook it loose and examined it. "Not a large parachute. Someone dropped a package—or something like that."

There was no package in the hole and I didn't expect to see one. That must have been picked up by whoever was expecting it. *This* was the buried evidence.

Here I was, I told myself, knee-high in mystery again, bewildered by clues—and close to the old inn, of course. I told myself I must find Mary and tell her of this latest development, and I comforted myself that she and her brother would know what to do.

"We must put it back," I said. Then, as Richard was prepared to argue, "No—I'm not taking it home! You know what happened to the ring Sally found! We don't want anyone else climbing in to get back what they've lost! *Leave it,* Richard!"

Richard was obviously at a loss to understand why, when I had taken all this trouble to find it, I was now prepared to leave this piece of evidence here in the woods. Still, he didn't argue and I knew why—because Peter Blake was mixed up in it and Richard was glad to let sleeping dogs lie. Carefully, we put the earth back over the square of silk and carefully I scattered twigs and leaves on top. It looked the same, I thought, as when Peter Blake had left it.

Neither of us was inclined to linger. We walked together through the wood looking much like Hansel and Gretel, I should think, with such a background, and in those costumes. But we didn't need pebbles or crumbs to show us where to go. Always, whatever we did, we were led back to The Silver Circle. There seemed no escape. To me, it began to appear like a nightmare whenever I thought of it.

We weren't going in, to-day, of course. Nothing would have made me—but I had to look up at it, as we passed. The windows on the ground floor were broken, with several panes missing, but in the upper rooms most of the windows were intact. I thought it might be made habitable, if enough hard work and money were spent on it. Then I remembered that Mary would not be living there after all. She had said she would like to make a home there —but it was most unlikely that, after all that had happened and would happen, she would be able to carry out her wish.

Thinking this, I stared at those upper windows, like eyes looking down at us. Then I stood still, feeling as if I were really in a nightmare. There was a man's face at one of those upper windows, near the bottom as though he were raising himself on his elbow, lying there, to look out. This was a room I remembered, from exploring the inn, as being small and dark and lonely . . .

The face, to me, seemed white and desperate-looking. Then, as we stared, it disappeared, suddenly. I didn't know if the man, who looked ill, hadn't the strength to go on sitting up or whether someone had pulled him back—I was ready to believe anything.

Richard and I stared at each other. His face was as frightened as mine. We didn't have to say, "Did you see who that was?"

It was the man we had found injured, on the rocks, who had so mysteriously disappeared!

CHAPTER EIGHT

THE SECRET OF THE INN

BY common but unspoken consent, it seemed that Richard and I had decided to say nothing about what we had seen.

But, when we arrived home that evening, there was another explanation to think up! *Sally* wanted to know why we had disappeared from the Carnival Parade! I decided to tell her just what had happened but to leave Mary Brown out of the story. "Where did the trail take you?" Sally asked, with the superior note in her voice that often moved me, not only to protest, but to downright anger. (Now though, I had to be careful not to antagonise Sally in case she told the grown-ups, so I swallowed my irritation.) But, when I said The Silver Circle, it was the best thing I could have said.

"*Oh!*" Sally's face became frozen over and she changed the subject.

We said nothing to Mummy and Martha, save that we hadn't got a prize. But, now that we had come home empty-handed, Martha was indignant and declared that the Tyrolean costumes *should* have won something.

"Maybe they weren't fancy enough?" she said. I was silent. Then, when it looked as though she might go further into the question, I dashed into a hurried and long description of the Orange and Lemon so that Martha forgot about us.

Next morning, I went to look for Mary Brown. I didn't know where to find her but, luckily, I saw her going into one of the shops in town, and waited for her to come out. She asked me to join her in morning coffee (only I, of course, had ice-cream) and while we sat there, in the café, I told her what had happened the day before. I think it made it easier for us both to talk of these fantastic happenings when we were in a crowd, with noise and bustle all round.

"Parachute silk?" Her face went pale as she said it. "What can it have been used for?" Her hands, I noticed, were trembling and she tried to hide them in her lap.

I didn't know. I couldn't even guess. I don't suppose Mary could either. One thing I *didn't* tell her—and that was about the man we had seen at the window of the inn. I don't know why—but somehow, I couldn't bring myself to mention it. It had given us such a bad shock and—if you stopped to think long over it—could conjure up such frightening thoughts that it was better pushed to the back of the mind and forgotten. I comforted myself that, soon, now, the authorities would work it all out . . .

That was what Mary said, at this moment—something like that. As she left, she said, gratefully, " It was clever of you, Livvy, to recognise Blake in the Parade. I knew you would be able to help, when I confided in you. I shall tell Hugh. The rest will be up to him—and he will know what to do. One thing I can promise—it won't be long now, before the whole affair is finished."

That was the best thing she could have told me for I was tired of all this mystery and of the name of The Silver Circle. I presumed, as I made my way home, that the investigators or whoever it was on the track of the wrong-doers, had gathered enough evidence and that the net was drawing in. One day, we should read of it, perhaps in the newspapers. But, if and when we did, I knew *I* shouldn't wish for any publicity—and I don't think Richard and Sally would either. Strangely, for we are a family where nothing is kept secret for long, everything that had happened had been successfully hidden from Mummy and Daddy. We hadn't meant to be so secretive but they had both been away from home at the time, and later, I felt I couldn't tell them anything. If I did, it might interfere with what Hugh Brown was doing. It was all very complicated and I knew they would not have approved if they had known how we were mixed up in these things—that was why it cheered me, now, to hear that the end was in sight. I hoped I could forget it as rapidly as I seemed to have been caught up in it.

The one thing we hadn't been able to hide, of course, was the accident to Sally's sketch—and that had been put down at last, after fruitless argument and explanation, as the work of some cruel and irresponsible person. We were reminded of what had happened later that day, when the results of the Art Competition were announced. I saw Sally glance down the list, quickly reading the names. I watched her. When she came to Kim's name, which would surely be there, I supposed she would redden and turn away. I know Sally still suspected that Kim had spoiled her drawing. Then I saw her frown and read through the names, again. She turned to me. "Kim didn't win."

"She probably didn't enter, after what happened to your drawing," I told her.

"But Livvy," Sally almost pleaded, "what else could have happened?"

"*I don't know,*" I said, as I had said all along. And, as I had also said, "But I do know *it wasn't Kim*."

I went alone to Judge Randall's house to see Kim. I think she knew, when she saw me, what I had come for. When we were alone, I tackled her about it. "You didn't send in your entry? You cancelled it?" I challenged.

She nodded impatiently, as though she wanted to

hear no more from anyone on the subject. I knew Sally would guess what Kim had done. Then, I told myself, she must feel ashamed of her suspicions.

"It's a funny thing," I said, knowing Kim wanted to change the subject, although I was not getting away from it altogether, "Peter Blake's painting of the inn was spoiled in much the same way."

She looked incredulous. "It was just like Sally's, wasn't it?"

"*Well*," I said, wanting to be fair to Sally, "it wasn't as good as hers. Nowhere near it. But I never like to criticise a person's drawings too much. They seem to get so attached to them—even the worst drawings."

"Blind spots," Kim agreed.

"But however bad it was," I went on, "I told him, at the time, it didn't deserve *that* fate!"

Kim asked me if he had any idea who could have done such a thing—but I told her he hadn't discussed a culprit with me—just shown me the picture.

"It's as if someone, hereabouts, doesn't want a painting of the old inn to be shown," Kim said, much as I had done. "As though they weren't taking the smallest chances, even in a local Art Competition." I may have looked startled at this flight of fancy for she laughed and said, "Only a wild guess, Livvy. If it were a mystery story and I the author, I should make them a gang of international smugglers, bringing in diamonds from Africa, and using the old inn as their secret headquarters. In that case, they would have to be careful no one suspected a thing! With sketches being made, right and left, they would become really annoyed.'' She looked at me. ''How's that for a plot?''

''Fine,'' I told her, and wondered what she would say if she knew how near she was to the truth. I longed to confide in her—Kim was so sensible and so matter-of-fact—she would take each fact, as it came, and each clue, marshalling them and finding which went after which . . . She would be the best help possible in unravelling a mystery. But again, my promise to Mary Brown came between us—and anyway, Kim had never liked Mary.

She went on. ''I'm plagued with mystery and wild guesses, this week! Shall I tell you what I concocted about the aeroplane and the racing car? Of course, there might be *nothing*—but that didn't satisfy *me*——''

''*What aeroplane? What car?*''

(More mystery—and from Kim, this time! I remembered Mary's words, ''It won't be long now,'' and had to ask myself if, by any chance, what Kim had to say was another part of *my* puzzle fitting in?)

We sat there, beneath the cedar on the lawn, and

she told me what had happened. The weather, for a few days, had been hot and sultry and Kim found that when she went to bed it was difficult to get to sleep.

I had to ask, as Richard undoubtedly would have asked, "What do you do, in Rhodesia, then?"

"There it doesn't come as such a shock," she told me, her eyes twinkling.

I let that pass.

"I was sitting on the window-seat in my room. The garden looked wonderful, Livvy—more beautiful, somehow, than the daylight colours. I heard an aeroplane pass low over the house. It sounded loud because everything was so still—but no one else seemed to have heard it. I asked, tentatively, next morning, but they all said no. It must have been a small machine—and it sounded so low, it might have landed somewhere on the Common. Then I heard the noise of a car, driven at terrific speed along the road. If P.C. Simms had been here, they wouldn't have gone far at that rate! The car was quite a long time after the plane . . . I wondered about them both, for a while, then went to bed. It was nearly three o'clock."

"Altogether a noisy night," I agreed. "And a late one."

Kim nodded. "I was prepared to forget about it, but it happened again, two night later."

"Couldn't you sleep *that* night?" I asked.

"I wasn't in bed," she said, her eyes dancing. "Sophie had had her puppies—and I just had to go down and see her! In the stables."

"*On your own?*" I asked.

She nodded. "Nothing to be scared of. Sophie seemed glad of company. She was all right so I didn't stay long. I heard the car again."

"How did you know it was the same car?"

"I didn't, of course. I just guessed it might be."

"What Richard would call a hunch?"

"That's it. It came up the lane at a tearing speed —and there are so few cars in the lane by day, let alone at night, that I had to investigate. Wouldn't you?" she asked me directly.

I didn't know. I decided to be honest. "No," I said. "Perhaps not. Not at that time."

"I was dressed," Kim said, simply, "so I followed it."

"But how did you know where to go?"

"It could only go on to the Common. The lane branches off, half a mile from here, and goes across the Common. That's why so few people take it, save those who want to picnic there. Certainly no one at night, unless——"

"Unless they were meeting someone, on the Common, at a secret rendezvous?" I finished for her, entering into the spirit of the thing.

"Exactly! That's what I thought and I just had to know. It wasn't dark because the moon lit up everything. I kept to the shadows myself, in case anyone saw *me*. I saw a car, parked at the side of the road. It was a black coupé and I went close enough to see the number. I could only see the shape of the driver's head from behind, when it drove off, across the Common. They must have used the headlights of the car to guide the aeroplane. The plane came in, some time later, but I had started for home then. Don't you think it was suspicious? Don't you think there was some connection?" she demanded.

I nodded. "What was the car number?" I asked, for I had suddenly had an idea. When she told me, I nodded. That was the number of Hugh Brown's car and I supposed he had used it for detecting work. I didn't tell Kim this and, when she continued to puzzle out *how* the aeroplane and the car might be connected, I turned the conversation, when I could, into safer channels.

Later we decided to take a walk through the woods. It was late afternoon and, when she suggested it, I knew where we should end. But I couldn't show too much to Kim the way I felt about the woods and The Silver Circle. I didn't want her to start guessing, for I had a feeling she wouldn't stop there. She wouldn't be content until she knew everything—and I wasn't in a position to tell her. Not yet.

When we did come to the inn, "Why do you look at it like that?" she said, eyeing me keenly. "As though you were reluctant to go in—as though you *know* something about the place?"

"Is that the way I look?" I made an effort to sound natural. "All right, let's go in. Let's make up a game about it! We never seem to play here. Sally used it as a model for her sketch—and the rest of us seemed to sit around and look at it! Let's go in—let's use it!" Then I added, prudently, "I have just half an hour before I have to start back."

"All right, Livvy." All the same, she looked strangely at me, as though she knew I was screwing up my courage, determined to come to grips with this place and what it was there that frightened me.

(If I really *romped* through it, I thought, putting its ghosts to flight, forgetting what I had been told was happening there, even to-day, I might get over my fear that something lay in wait for me. It was a feeling I couldn't explain away and, since I couldn't rid myself of it by staying safely outside, I determined to go in and see if I couldn't forget it, at least for a time.)

We decided we were heiresses, Kim and I, making a journey by coach, putting up at The Silver Circle for the night. Kim wondered if it wouldn't be more exciting to be heiresses running away—running off to marry a handsome Captain of the Guard or from an over-strict uncle—but I wouldn't have this! "We are making a safe, quite ordinary journey from one country seat to another," I explained. "No incidents—no adventures . . ."

She looked disappointed, but I was firm and went on, "We are putting up at The Silver Circle, which is a respectable, highly-thought-of inn, recommended by all those who make the journey along this road."

"What about the horses?" she said, as I knew she would.

I told her the horses had been seen to—the servant girl was this minute putting a warming-pan in the bed.

"Not in summer!" Kim protested.

"To air the sheets, at any time," I told her, firmly. "Besides, a warming-pan is so decorative."

Kim told me that was when they hung on walls, in the twentieth century. If Sally could have heard us, she would have dismissed all this as childish, in spite of the fact that she is younger than we are. But, when you are in the mood for make-believe, nothing is more fun—and we were in the mood. I was glad to imagine the inn as it had been once—a busy, bustling place, alive with people . . .

We played our game out, sweeping with a flurry of skirts across the threshold, calling imperiously for the host. But I wouldn't let Kim go off on her own. With her for company, I didn't find the place so frightening. But there was still something lurking at the back of my mind that worried me. When

I had planned the game, I had no intention of going *upstairs* for I remembered the man's face we had seen, Richard and I, at the window—the man we had seen, once before, lying unconscious on the cliff. What if he—or anyone—were still there? I told myself that he couldn't be—we should have seen evidences—*but what if he were*?

When Kim started up the stairs, I caught her arm. "Not up there! Stay here!"

"But we mean to sleep here! We can't do that, on the ground floor! Besides, I want to look for a secret panel!"

Helplessly, I stared at her, wondering what mystery this was.

"For my jewels," she told me reasonably. "If I'm an heiress, I have jewels which I carry round in a small brass-bound box—carved, with a handle. They always did it, or gave them to their maids to carry. We haven't any maids. I want to put my jewel box safely away—and there must be a panel in one of the bedrooms. There were always secret panels. They went with all the best inns—they were never built without them!"

After that, there was nothing I could do save follow her up the stairs. Of course, the room she chose was the one I feared—but I saw the door was open and breathed with relief. "Come in," Kim called, over her shoulder. "There's no one here. It's reserved for us!"

At the doorway I still hesitated. I looked round. Dust and cobwebs . . . a dirty window . . . shadows already gathering in the corners . . . But no sign that anyone had been here.

Kim was still determined to find the secret panel and went round knocking the walls. But she was disappointed. Not one of them sounded hollow. Then I told her *my* fancy was for loose floor-boards. If ever I had treasure to hide—which was most unlikely, either now or a hundred years ago—it would be beneath a floor-board. I said this with such emphasis that Kim stopped her tapping to ask me why.

"For the joy of having people walk over it, not knowing it was there!"

She agreed that such a feeling would indeed make one feel clever. "But if you don't take care," she warned, "you'll go right through! The floorboards aren't too safe. And the dust you are moving! Look at that pile there!"

I looked where she pointed. "I didn't do that," I protested. "I haven't been in that corner."

Slowly, I walked towards it, and stared. "But someone has," I said. *"Recently!"* Something in my voice made Kim look up. When she saw the way I looked, she came across and stood by my side and looked down with me. The dust was plainly disturbed. One floorboard, near the wall, was swept clean, while nearby was the accumulation of years.

I remembered what I had said, "if I had something to hide, I should put it beneath a floorboard." Had someone else been here, with the same thoughts? I remembered again the man's face, at the window . . .

"Livvy, how clever you are! There is something hidden here. There must be." Kim's voice quivered with excitement. "Jewels, after all?"

I had to remind her the dust had been disturbed *recently*. "Not an heiress's jewels," I said. "Something was hidden here—or taken away—only a few days ago." Then, as she turned away, I said, "What are you going to do?"

She was looking round for something with which to prise up the floorboard. I had a penknife in the pocket of my blazer. I handed it to her. She slipped it between the boards and carefully worked it round. The board was loose, no question of that. I stooped and helped her pull it up. Then I knelt beside her and, "Careful," I said, when I saw her put her hand down. I saw by her face she had found something. She brought up a package wrapped in oiled silk.

It wasn't over-large but I stared at it as though it might bite her. "Open it!" I said. *I* couldn't do much. My hands were shaking too much to be of help.

Slowly and carefully, she unwrapped the silk. I could see she felt nothing save curiosity and excitement but I felt again the fear that came to me whenever I thought of this place. I wanted to say, "Kim, no! Put it back. Let's go——" But it was too late. She was already showing me what was inside the package. Neat piles of bank-notes, clean and fresh, obviously unused. I didn't touch them, not even by a finger. Neither did Kim. She put them on the dirty floor, between us, and we stared, fascinated.

"What shall we do?" My voice was a whisper though, as far as we knew, there was no one to hear.

Kim's voice, when she replied, was calm and clear. "Take them to the police. There must have been a robbery."

I had to admire her coolness though I didn't know if she felt that way, inside. I was shaking. This, then, was the end of the clues, the hints, the strange premonition I had had that there was something sinister going on at the inn. Its secret was out, at last, in this haul of stolen bank notes.

Then I said, "If they are stolen?"

"What do you mean?"

"Counterfeit," I suggested, for the idea had just come to me.

Kim's eyes narrowed. "They may be. Anyway, let's go to the police."

Carefully, we replaced the floorboard, exactly as we had found it, then went silently down the stairs, all thoughts of make-believe gone for good. Even Kim, now, seemed awed by what had happened. I know her face was paler than usual and she crept ahead of me, as quietly as she could. When we got outside, I was surprised to see the sun shining and everything bright and normal.

At the door of the inn, Kim turned and faced me. "Livvy, this is serious. More than we guess, I suppose. I think we should separate. You go and tell your father. Tell him everything, quickly, then he'll know just what to do. I'll go a different way, into town, and tell the police."

I didn't want us to separate, not for a minute. But I could see she meant it. She didn't wait for me to answer but was off through the trees. I turned and ran off, myself, as fast as I could, jumping over scrub, skirting tree-trunks, all the time trying to get my story properly phrased and ready to tell Daddy, as soon as I found him. I didn't want to waste time when I got there, and it was a story so difficult to believe that it would need the minimum of words and exact marshalling of facts.

Then I heard someone following me. Twigs snapped and bushes rustled. You can't be absolutely silent, in a wood. I thought maybe Kim was coming after me, after all. But, when I turned, it was Mary Brown, standing almost behind me.

I didn't know, when I considered Mary such a good friend, why I should have felt frightened to see her.

But I did. I felt a sudden sharp *jab* of fright, as

if something really had injured me. Perhaps it was
because of the way I was keyed up after our dis-
covery. Perhaps it was because Mary, too, looked
different. She didn't look as she had done, when we
first met her, nor even when she told me her story
and asked for my help. She looked cold and unfriendly, not like Mary at all. But because she was
Mary, and I trusted her, I told her all that had happened—about Kim and I finding the money—and
now Kim had gone one way and I was going to tell
my father and get the help of the authorities . . . I
thought she would be delighted to hear it because
even I could see it must be connected with what her
brother was doing and would help settle the case,
perhaps sooner than she hoped.

But she didn't smile. She waited for me to finish.
Then she said, standing blocking my path towards
the edge of the wood, "But you aren't going into
town and you won't tell anyone—not until *we* let
you go. You are coming with me." She spoke in a
flat, expressionless tone, so unlike the way she
usually sounded that I could only stare at her. I
didn't understand what she meant. I heard the
words but they had no meaning, made no sense.
She sounded like an enemy—*Mary*—whom I had
liked and trusted, who had always been so friendly,
who had told me so much. She had confided in me
so that I was sorry for her and had promised to
help . . .

I didn't move. Her grip tightened on my arm. She didn't hurt me but I knew, then, that she was serious.

I looked down at her fingers, as they closed round my arm, and what I saw there confirmed all I was thinking, and I knew Mary was not what I had thought her to be—and never had been.

On the middle finger of her right hand she wore a silver ring. It was a ring with which I had grown familiar—a ring I could easily recognise, now. It was like the ring Sally had found and taken home, and lost again—a ring I had seen on the finger of the injured man on the cliff.

("What if there is a connection?" Sally had teased. "A connection between the inn and the ring —*two Silver Circles*?")

Of course, there was a connection—a sinister connection—and Mary Brown was concerned in it. What, then, did that make her—and what would happen to me?

CHAPTER NINE

INTO THE CAVE

I WONDERED if Mary Brown guessed my thoughts as I stared so hard at the ring. If she did, she showed nothing, but, still with that pressure on my arm, turned me in the direction from which I had come —towards the inn. There was nothing I could do save go with her and I am afraid I had no heroic thoughts of trying to run away or of suddenly breaking loose and twisting and turning through the trees. Nothing like that—for I felt dazed, not able to think clearly save of one thing—that, whatever was going on at The Silver Circle, Mary was one of those who were doing wrong. She was not on the side of authority—she wasn't the person she had all along pretended to be—and she had deliberately and cruelly deceived and used me.

We went inside the inn, and I thought of the time, some half-hour before, when Kim and I had played happily, with no thought of anything like this.

Mary took little notice of me once we were there. She took me with her up to the room where Kim and I had found the money and I saw her lips tighten as she saw the loose floorboard and the dark hole beneath. I sat on the window-seat. It was hard and it was dirty. The windows, too, were dusty, but I rubbed clear one of the upper panes, and stared out. That was where I should be, out there, on my way to Fold, ready to tell my story, seeking help. I kept my head lifted up high and turned away from Mary Brown. For all I was upset and the first stirrings of fear made me wish I was anywhere, save here, I wasn't going to let her see me cry!

I didn't know what was going to happen. I had been so thoroughly deceived in her, I didn't know what to think. I supposed she must be waiting for her brother, and I supposed they would keep me locked here, while they made their get-away. If they did, I should only be a short time on my own. Kim knew where I was and Kim would bring the police back with her. Probably, if Hugh Brown didn't turn up very soon, Kim and the police would be here before Mary got away. This was the way I thought, not anticipating I should have to stay here long. Anyway, I told myself, even *ghosts*, now, would be preferable to real people whom you had trusted, then found they had betrayed you, and made your world come tumbling down about your ears.

Then another thought came . . . what if Mary and her brother took me with them? I tried not to think of that because it would mean I might end up *anywhere*, away from home and friends and with no hope of getting in touch with them. But I didn't think this would happen. If they planned to get away quickly, now that everything was discovered, they would not want to be saddled with a third person—and they were leaving, that was plain. Mary had a brief-case, open in front of her, where she sat on an old broken backless chair, and she leafed through a pile of papers, putting them into bundles, leaving some out. She frowned as she went through them, biting her lip, and this made me feel better. Once, when I glanced at her, I found she was looking at me. I stared steadily back. I didn't think of her, now, as a person I had known and liked. She was someone who had told untruths and was not to be trusted. She said, softly, "Where did the other girl take the money, Livvy?"

"*To the police,*" I said, my voice over-loud in that quiet room. It didn't quiver though. I was proud of that. In fact, it sounded defiant.

She shook her head. "She hasn't a chance of doing that. It was stupid of you to get mixed up in this. We didn't want to harm you. But wherever *I* was, *you* seemed to turn up, with your stories of what had happened and what you had stumbled on. If you had gone away from here that first day, you would have known nothing, guessed nothing, and it would have been safer for you."

I didn't answer and silence lay heavy on the room. She sat, staring in front of her, and I asked myself, indignantly, how I was expected to know, in the beginning, what was going to happen? I was in the habit of believing people to be whom they said they were! The inn had stood, for as long as anyone could remember, deserted and forlorn. How were we to guess it had suddenly become—and at a time when my sister Sally decided to sketch it— the headquarters of a gang of . . . *what?* Smugglers? Thieves? I still didn't know . . .

Time dragged. I wondered how much longer it would be before Kim came back with help. I supposed she would telephone my father and, when she found I hadn't been home, would bring help and come searching for me. As though she read my thoughts, Mary said, ''She won't get there—that other girl. We knew you were here. There are hiding-places in this inn you know nothing about. We knew you had found the money, though we couldn't stop you, *then*. But we never meant you to get away with it. We saw you start off, in different directions. Clever of you, Livvy. But we are two, as well. *Hugh followed your friend.* He'll find her. He won't let her get away.''

So my hopes crashed round me. Kim might be clever and resourceful but she was no match for a grown man, and one desperate at the thought of his plans being dashed—plans which had taken weeks to perfect and which we had stumbled on at the end . . . No thief nor smuggler was going to let her get away to the police with her story without doing everything he could to prevent her.

Minutes were like hours, there in that room . . . but surely, I thought, if Hugh Brown were in pursuit of Kim, he would have found her by now. Had she got through? Had she managed to get to the main road and been given a lift by a car into Fold? It was an hour since I had been shut up here, with Mary Brown.

The shadows were lengthening and I turned my back on the window, preferring to stare sullenly at the opposite wall. I would not meet Mary's eyes and I did not wish to speak to her. The wood, outside the window, seemed to be creeping closer in the dark, as though, when night came, the inn would be swallowed up and hidden . . . I shivered but fortunately Mary didn't see me.

I was hungry and, by now, frightened. I had to admit it.

The one thing that cheered me was that Mary was obviously restless and frightened, too. She continually glanced at her watch. She crossed to the window and peered out, above my head. When she came near me, I turned away. Then she would go back to the old chair and sit there, nervously going through her papers for a second and third time. The way she acted encouraged me to hope.

Then my heart and my hopes went crashing again . . .

There was a noise downstairs, a pause and a scuffle, then the door of the room where we sat burst open. Hugh Brown was there, with Kim. When I saw her, the tears I had so long held back really did come though I swallowed hard and pretended they weren't there. I had pinned everything on Kim getting through to the police and I didn't dare ask myself what would happen now. Kim gave me a gay and cheerful smile, to which I returned a watery one.

She didn't look miserable or defeated but she was certainly dishevelled. Bits of leaf and twigs stuck to her clothes. There were smudges of mud and dirt on her arms and legs and a tear in one sleeve. But now that I did see her and had her here for company, I was selfish enough to feel a surge of relief and gladness. Even though hopes of escape seemed to have gone, nothing would seem so bad with Kim there. She came coolly across the room, and, "Move up, Livvy," she said. Her voice didn't shake one little bit.

I listened while Hugh Brown told his sister, quickly, angrily, what had happened. It seemed Kim had eluded him for a long time in the woods. He hadn't been able to catch her and it was only by an unlucky fall and the noise she made that he had found her again, and this time she hadn't got away. When he did catch her, the notes were not on her. She had had time, by twisting and doubling back, to hide them, and nothing Hugh could say or threaten would make her tell him where they were hidden.

He didn't threaten us very much, but, for my part, he didn't have to. The coldness with which he spoke was sufficient to make me shiver, the look in his eyes and the set of his mouth. It was plain Mary was more frightened than ever and the cool way in which Kim stared back at her and the indifference with which she listened, seemed to exasperate Mary to breaking-point. She said, desperately, "Hugh, we must go! We have so little time—and we can't keep them waiting."

He said, savagely, "We can't meet them without the money, either. There's time. Don't panic. We shall find it."

Kim started to whistle—a gay little tune which I had heard her whistle often, before. Mary looked as though she would like to scream at her to stop. I saw her hands clench at her sides. Her brother took hold of her arm and led her to the door. They went out, closing it behind them. As I watched, I saw something I had overlooked previously. The lock on the door was shining new. Obviously, it had only lately been put on and I thought instantly of the man Richard and I had seen imprisoned in this room. He, too, had been connected with The Silver Circle but not on the side of Hugh and Mary Brown! I wouldn't think how he had got from the cliffs near the Letty farm to this deserted place—I didn't want to frighten myself unnecessarily—but I could give a guess who was responsible—and for the "accident". In spite of making a tremendous effort to be as brave and outwardly nonchalant as Kim, I shivered when I thought to what lengths these people would go. But then, Kim didn't know anything about the man on the cliff . . . As Mary had said, *I* was the one who knew most of the story for I seemed to be the link between the episodes. I know I would gladly have given that position to someone else!

We heard voices rising and falling, outside the door. One low, authoritative, evidently Hugh's— the other inclined to rise shrilly and hysterically. "She's getting scared," Kim said, with satisfaction.

I didn't ask her what she had done with the money because I honestly did not want to know. "Don't worry, Livvy," she said. "Everything will be all right." I hoped she was as sure as she sounded.

I saw her idly drawing on the dust of the window-pane and envied the calm way she took things!

Then the door opened and Mary Brown came in. She went swiftly to where she had left the brief-case, opened it (to see if we had meddled, I suppose), then back again to the door. When she reached it, she stood there, her hand on the handle. Almost, she seemed to be drawing attention to the door.

"Livvy," she started to say, then shrugged, and left the room. We heard her brother's voice, savagely clear. "All right, then. I suppose we must go! The car is waiting at the bridge. Have you brought everything?"

We flattened our faces against the window-pane, staring out into the gathering dusk. We saw them go off between the trees, each carrying a suitcase. Only then did we jump up, the same thought in our minds. Kim put it into words. "She didn't lock the door!"

(I asked myself if Mary had done this *purposely*? Had she wanted me to escape, after all? Was it on her conscience that I should have been caught up in all this, through no fault of my own, and was she trying to get me out? Somehow, even now, I found it difficult to believe these terrible things of Mary Brown—that she had been, all the time, a criminal. I think I preferred to believe that she was trying to help us . . .)

But Kim wasted no time worrying about Mary Brown's conscience. Gently, she opened the door. The creak it made sounded like a scream, there in that quiet place. She looked out. I was so close behind her that, if she had turned suddenly, I should have toppled backwards. She tiptoed out and down the stairs, with me still close behind. The stairs groaned and creaked. I don't know what I expected to pounce out and put a hand on my shoulder! Nothing happened. We got safely down to the passage leading through the ground floor from front to back. The door was open and there, some yards away, the wood began. When we got through that to the other side, we should be very close to safety.

Yet, at the moment, I hesitated, fearing it might be a trap. I held Kim's arm. "Don't go," I said involuntarily.

"What is it, Livvy? We must go. We can't waste time." She pulled me with her, almost roughly, in her haste. We dashed across the empty stretch of grass and into the shelter of the trees. No voice called after us. No hand stretch out to stop us so that I began to believe that, after all, I had escaped—thanks to Mary. But I said, urgently, "Kim, this time I can't go off without you. I can't go through the wood on my own. Whatever happens, we must stay together." She could think me the worst coward, but that was the truth and that was the way I felt. I would stick close to her, whatever she did and wherever she went, but I could not make another journey beneath those darkening trees on my own.

"Of course we stay together," she said. "Come on!"

We started to run, skirting the bushes, jumping them where they were low, and, where nothing else could be done, struggling through thorns and briar, with the worst results to our clothes!

"*Where* did you hide it?" I gasped—and gasped again when she told me.

"Beneath the waterfall!"

I could see, now, that we were going in the direction of The White Veil. I could hear its noise, growing clearer and louder. When we got to the bank there was no one in sight. Kim turned to me and said, swiftly and directly, "Livvy, what shall we do? Leave it—go and tell the police and let them come back and look for it? *Or get it?*" I knew what she wanted me to say and it was what *I* wanted to say—and do. After all we had gone through, I didn't want to be cheated of any glory due to us.

"We'll go and get it ourselves!" I said, firmly.

"Good for you!" Kim told me.

It *was* the way I felt. Our story could not be complete if we had no evidence to show! I felt, somehow, that to take the bundle of notes from here and give them ourselves into the safe keeping of the police would repay the Browns for what they had done—and the fright they had given *me*, at any rate!

We had to shout to make ourselves heard above the noise of the falling water. (That was why we didn't hear the other noise—of someone following us. . . .)

Kim started slithering down the bank. I made to follow but was slower than she and was still near the top of the bank when I heard a voice. (I nearly fell headlong into the water and had to grab an out-thrust arm of shrub!) "It worked, then?" the voice said. "This was the spot where I lost her before. I searched, everywhere, but couldn't believe she would have gone down to the river. There's no path. I couldn't make out where she had been."

"It must be here. They must know of some place not easy to find." The second voice I heard clearly, too, and it was just as familiar.

I stayed there, out of sight from the top of the bank, my feet on a slippery hold but just managing to keep myself from falling into the water, and I thought bitterly how we had been tricked. Then, once and for all, any thoughts I might have had that Mary Brown was sorry for what she had done and wished to make amends went out of my mind. *Of course,* the door of the room at the inn had been purposely left unlocked so that Kim and I could "escape" and, unsuspectingly, lead Mary Brown and her brother to where Kim had hidden the money. It was a simple plan but it had worked well. How I regretted now that I hadn't advised Kim to go straight to Fold and the police!

I didn't know what to do and I tried to think faster than ever in my life before. Kim was already below and, any moment, she would call up, in her clear, far-carrying voice, "Livvy, here I am! What are you doing—come on down!" That would give everything away and lead them to her, at once.

I crept along the bank, holding on to the scrub, desperately trying to find a foothold, collecting scratches and rents. (I didn't, for a moment, stop to ask myself what would be the outcome of all this when I got home. There was enough trouble in it, now, for me, without looking to the future! But, when I had escaped safely from this evening's escapade, there would be Daddy and Mummy to face . . . *and Martha*!)

I went some way along the bank, hoping they wouldn't see me. Then I called, *" Kim—here!"* loud enough for them to hear.

My plan worked, as theirs had. I heard them run from where they were standing, along the top of the bank to where I was at the moment. The ferns and scrub hid me from view and, still crouching, I went back, as fast as I could, and down to where Kim waited at the bottom. It was only a simple ruse and I knew it wouldn't hold them off for long. Once they got to the bottom of the bank they were bound to find us, but I hoped it would work long enough for me to get to Kim and tell her what had happened—that we had been followed and the Browns were with us again. At least, there might be time for her to find another safer hiding place for the money. *That*, I knew, was what they wanted and they were not prepared to go off without it.

I found Kim waiting anxiously at the bottom, wondering why I had taken so long. I held on to her arm, while the water fell in a shining arc above us, and gasped out what had happened.

"It's what they would do!" she said. "They are desperate for the money! They must be afraid to meet whoever it is, empty-handed. There's only one thing." She stopped and looked over her shoulder.

"I thought of that too," I said. "The cave leads into a passage. We wouldn't explore it that afternoon we were here. I didn't say *why* . . . because we were afraid to . . ."

"Then the time has come," Kim said grimly. "Hurry, Livvy! We can hide there, at least—and follow it to the end if we have to! It must come out somewhere."

"What if it's a dead end?" I had to ask, but Kim shook her head. "Don't think that way."

We went across the ledge, beneath the falling water, and into the mouth of the cave.

I remembered clearly that previous afternoon when we had no wish to enter it. Then the sun was shining and everything was normal. How different now—darkness all round, and two desperate people pursuing us! The thought of following that dark, damp passage to goodness-knows-where, at such a time, seemed the last straw and, even now, I hesitated. Kim gave me a tug. "It's that or have the Browns catch up with us," she said.

Then, "They've found a way down!" I gasped. I could hear Hugh Brown call out to his sister.

Stones came rattling down the bank to fall into the water.

We had no torch, nothing to help or guide us, but without a thought we plunged into the darkness of the cave. There was dim grey light for a few yards, then darkness, thick and complete. It was damp underfoot. Water dripped on to the floor and on to us. We splashed through pools and soon my shoes were heavy and wet. But I suppose fright gave us courage for we ran on. We could hear voices plainly now, from behind us. They had found the mouth of the cave and were catching up.

"In here—I can hear them!" Hugh Brown called out and, when I looked back once, I made out a pin-prick of light which must have been their torch. Kim clutched a parcel under her arm. She had had it with her since we came into the cave but I hadn't commented on it because I knew what it was—the money which was the cause of all the trouble.

I knew something else, too. If the Browns caught up with us now, and we gave them the money, they would not let us go. We knew too much. It was better that we went on, trying to escape—trying to get the evidence and the spoils away from these two who followed us and who wanted it so desperately.

CHAPTER TEN

BACK AT THE SILVER CIRCLE

I HAD never been anywhere as dark nor as smothering as that passage! We didn't run for long—we couldn't—but we had almost to feel our way. Our pursuers had a torch, of course, so could make better speed. The passage seemed to go on and on, turning and winding, and, as we followed it, I only hoped it came up, somewhere! Kim kept firm hold of my arm and that comforted me—the satisfaction of knowing that we were in this together. I could never have done it on my own. I think I should have turned and made my way back to the Browns rather than go on!

Then Kim said, "Light ahead—*there*! I knew we should make it, Livvy! We may be safe, yet." I didn't say what I was thinking—that the Browns might, in the open, on level ground, stand a better chance of catching up with us. As if she guessed my anxious thoughts, Kim said, "We may meet someone with a car. Don't give up hope! Do you know where we might be?"

I had no idea. What had happened this evening

had put all clear, sensible thoughts well out of my head and I couldn't stop to work out the geography of the place. "Somewhere on the moor?" I ventured. That was all I could do.

Somehow, though, that blue of light did give us hope. We had successfully eluded the Browns and left them behind, so far, and we were only two young girls against a man and his sister. We might, as Kim hoped, come up somewhere near the main road, where we could hail a passing car, and the Browns, if they valued their skins, would have to make off. But not for long! *Now* I should have no feelings at all about telling everything I knew to the police and putting them on the track of the criminals. Thinking this way, bubbling over with righteous indignation, I forgot to feel frightened!

The light grew clearer as we neared the opening. But the sound of the Browns on our tracks grew louder too. I didn't know what would happen first —would we safely get out into the open—or would they catch up with us?

"I'm not going to give up, easily, without a fight!" Kim said, grimly, hitching the parcel tighter under her arm.

Then—suddenly—we stopped where we were, unable to move, and I had my worst fright of all that evening! What I had felt, before, was nothing to the fear that kept me rooted to the spot! Kim's hand froze on my arm and she held me so tight that I found, next day, I was bruised. We both stood, unable to move. The light we had been making for was cut off as if a shade had been pulled down over it. There was darkness behind us, and darkness ahead. The Browns were behind us too, but, for the moment, I almost preferred *them*. At least, I knew them. They were familiar.

A figure stood at the mouth of the cave—a shapeless figure in clothes that flapped round it. It looked strange and menacing and I had never seen anything like it for I never have nightmares. If I did, I know I should see something like this in one! It did not seem like an ordinary person, yet I knew it must be . . . and . . . *"Tramps,"* I whispered. I am afraid I did sob, then. I couldn't help it. To think our evening had ended like this. We had— and without boasting, I could say it—satisfactorily held our own against the Browns and stood a good chance—if we got out of this awful passage—of foiling them and dashing to safety. Now, the mouth of the passage, our only means of escape, was blocked. We were caught between two people whom we knew to be our enemies and this strange, frightening figure . . .

"What is it?" Kim whispered. I noticed she didn't say *"who"*.

But she might have done—for the figure at the

mouth of the cave said a strange and comforting thing. It might look like a scarecrow or something out of a dream, after too much supper, but what it said was, *"Come on, Livvy. Get behind me!"*

I didn't move. I was rooted to the spot by fear and bewilderment. Kim was quicker to recognise the voice. "Livvy," she yelled. "Isn't it the artist —the man who can't paint pictures?"

"Peter Blake!"

I said the name, aloud, and, "That's it! *Quick*," he said, again, coming nearer. He took hold of me, for he seemed to understand I couldn't move, and pushed me towards the opening. He called to some-one outside, "Look after the children." Vaguely, I knew he meant us but I was too dazed to object. I sat down, suddenly. I hoped no one would speak to me for I couldn't answer. But, for once, even Kim was silent. She sat next me, and put her arm round my shoulders.

"Two girls—two *little* girls!" a voice said, as though we were strange creatures out of some fabulous tales. "In that passage, with the others."

"Not *with* them," Kim protested. "Running away, as fast as we could!" She gave a laugh then that sounded more like her usual self—and weakly, I joined in.

The policeman who bent over us and shone his torch into our faces was elderly and comforting. To me, he looked like Saint George must have looked to many a maiden on being rescued from the dragon!

"See that they get home safely," Peter Blake called out. Then, quickly, "Who drew the water-fall on the window? You deserve a medal for quick thinking——"

It wasn't easy to see if Kim blushed. When I fully understood what he meant, I knew *I* thought her the cleverest girl alive! When we had been sitting there, imprisoned by Mary Brown, I had noticed Kim idly drawing on the window-pane. At least, that was what I thought—what she really did was draw a quick sketch, in the dust on the glass, of the water-fall, with the name beneath, hoping that whoever was on the track of the Browns—and it was plain the end was in sight—would come into this room, see what she had done, and know what it meant. She had pinned a lot on the other person being a quick thinker, too! *"Oh, Kim!"* I said, but she wouldn't let me say more.

"It was just a chance! When I did it, I didn't think anything would happen. It's Mr. Blake we must congratulate."

"I will," I said, "when we see him again."

At the moment, our Mr. Blake was busy pursu-ing the Browns through the passage, in the oppo-site direction from the one they had pursued us—and I was certain he didn't mean to let them go! I began to lose the frightened feeling—and to feel very, very tired.

It had been a long and arduous evening.

Sergeant Penn took us in the car, back to Judge Randall's house. Kim and her grandfather urged me to stay the night and I was tempted to—but reluctantly, had to refuse. It wasn't that I so much wished to spend a night away from home but I wasn't anxious to go home to Fold and face the family! But it had to be done. Daddy came racing out, once he heard the story, to see if I was all right—then raced off again, after telling me to go back—Mummy was waiting!

To-night, I suppose he hadn't had time to consider *my* part in all this. To-morrow, and at his leisure, he would want to know more.

I went home in the Judge's car, and, when I was safely delivered on the step, Mummy acted in much the same way as Daddy. She took one look at me and, though her lips tightened, and I knew that, some time soon, I would be in for the biggest row yet—evidently it wasn't to be *to-night*! "You are to sleep in the spare room," she told me. Not because I was being punished, I thought, but because Mummy didn't want Sally and Richard to keep me awake all night, talking. Mummy needn't have bothered. I was asleep in an instant. I went on sleeping, as Sally told me, wrathfully, as though I had been sleepless for *nights*—for she had looked in, at intervals, next morning, and there I was, deaf to her whispered, "Livvy, tell us about it!"

When I did wake, the first thing I thought of was the parcel of notes. I couldn't remember what had happened to them and the thought stayed with me and plagued me so that there was just one thing to do. I dressed and tiptoed down into the hall. I telephoned Kim and, when I asked her, she said, "I gave them to Peter Blake, when we passed him at the mouth of the cave. Livvy, are you in disgrace?"

"I have a feeling I am," I said. "But I haven't seen anyone yet. What about you?"

"Grandfather is torn between wanting to cable Rhodesia, complaining about my foolishness—and chuckling over what happened to the Browns!"

The headlines in Daddy's paper gave us an outline of what happened and we learned, too, that the person we knew as Peter Blake was a special investigator with great experience and an enviable reputation. Richard looked at me, as we read this —but I dared him to comment! "Haul of Counterfeit Notes" . . . "Round-Up of Criminal Organisation" . . . I had the feeling, as I read, that it had been a play and I had taken part in it—for what should *Livvy Taylor* be doing, mixed up in a criminal organisation? (That was what Daddy and Mummy—and Martha!—wanted to know too!)

I read with pleasure every detail of the Browns'

arrest. The story went on to describe their career. Most of it had taken place in South America but not as Mary had told me. What the paper didn't describe was the way they were caught, soaked to the skin when they fell into the river, running away from the police! That was a piece of news Sergeant Penn passed on to me, and which I was very pleased to hear and pass on to the others. "Soaked, they were," he said, with relish. "And serves 'em right! But wet or not," he added, with satisfaction, "we took 'em!"

On the evening of the day following our escapade, Sally and Richard and I were interviewed, too—by our parents. The door was carefully shut against possible intrusion, and we stood in a row, opposite Mummy and Daddy, while we got the dressing-down of our lives. When that was over, Mummy could not help but add hair-raising descriptions of what might have happened to us—children as we were—getting mixed up with such people!

It was no use us trying to say, "But, Mummy, it didn't happen." I have noticed before that interruptions of this kind make grown-ups worse! "To think . . ." Mummy would say, while we stood, heads bowed, able to do nothing save listen. (I told myself that if such things had really happened, as Mummy described, then we should indeed have merited a row! They hadn't—here we were, safe and sound—but we were getting it, anyway!)

We were told that we should have informed a responsible person, at once, when we found the ring—and when we lost it.

"A burglary!" Mummy shuddered. "Here, in the house, and I knew nothing."

"Mummy, you weren't here!" Sally protested. "And I had to go there again—I had to finish my sketch. Though I needn't have done it, as it turned out," she muttered.

Mummy told us a great deal about "evading the issue"—and we were made to promise that, never again, under any circumstances, would we carry on alone.

At last, we were allowed to leave and, as we did, I heard Mummy say, "Can you imagine . . . children like that . . . so deeply involved . . ."

I knew it would take her a long time—and take us even longer, on our best behaviour—to get over what had happened, now.

We went into the garden—very shaken, I must admit. Sally wiped her eyes, her back turned to us, and I had to swallow hard. Richard, after a moment's scowling into space, said, "What they don't understand is that *we* have feelings, too! We like to follow things through and see if we can't work them out and get the better of them. All that mystery, up there at the inn, was infuriating, but it was exciting—you must admit that! One got a thrill from it—and we couldn't always be running to the nearest grown-up when something extra-ordinary happened.''

I agreed with him but not wholly about the thrill. There had been times when I had got much more than a thrill—when I had been downright scared. It had been easy for me to promise not to get mixed up in anything like this again. I didn't want to . . .

Richard went on, arguing the case to his own satisfaction, ''We shall never grow up—and that's what they are always urging us to do!—if we keep going to them with every little problem! They can't have it both ways.''

'''Self-reliance,' they say, on the one hand,'' I agreed, carrying on for him, '' and 'How could you be so fool-hardy?', on the other.''

Richard looked at me admiringly. We were feeling better and more united every minute. There is *nothing* so one-sided as having to stand up to massed grown-up attack.

''And it isn't as if we deliberately got ourselves mixed up in it,'' Sally said. ''We were just there, when the clues were! We couldn't avoid them.''

So that we went into supper, feeling much the same as usual. We went to bed, feeling worse than ever . . . *Martha* had had her say in the meantime!

The next day, and the next, we had to bottle up any wish to discuss the Silver Circle for we received no encouragement when we did. As is the way of news, the episode was not reported again in the newspapers so that we were left, high and dry, wondering and surmising. We knew, more or less, what the end would be—what we wanted to know was how it started—and where—and when . . . how the ends, those infuriating ends that *we* could not tie up, knitted together . . . ends hanging out, in the untidiest way, as Sally put it!

"Do you know everything?" I asked Daddy, one evening. I couldn't keep silent any longer.

He put down his paper, glanced at me, then laughed. He didn't have to ask, "Everything about what?" He said, "Poor Livvy, it *is* a shame! You deserve to know *all* the story, if only for the fright it gave you!"

I stared back, saying nothing, in case what I said was the wrong thing—but hoping, all the time . . .

"Why not go up there to-morrow?" Daddy suggested. "Maybe you'll find your story, waiting to be finished off."

"*To the inn!* Do you mean it?"

"There's nothing there to hurt you now. But remember, if you see anything that looks remotely like a mystery——"

"I'll run for my life!" I promised, eagerly. "Richard and Sally, too."

I telephoned Kim and asked her if she would meet us at the inn. She said she had planned to go there herself—so it seemed as if we were meant to meet there that afternoon. (Of course, I didn't know then that this was really so . . . that Daddy and Judge Randall and another third person had got together and decided we should pay one last visit to The Silver Circle. I only understood this later!)

Kim was already there when we arrived, and we sat, the four of us, on the grass in front of the inn and stared at it. I suppose we were each thinking different thoughts—no two people think the same way, even about the same things—but I was certain we were all thinking along the same lines—of the fantastic use to which this derelict old place had been put. Now it dreamed there, quiet and forlorn . . .

"Quite deserted," Sally said, with a sigh. I don't think she sighed because she was sorry it was quiet but there was some feeling about the place that depressed you. I had always found it so—now, it seemed the others inclined that way. I know none of us wanted to go any nearer.

Then Richard said, "It isn't deserted. *There's smoke coming from the chimney!*"

For a full minute we stared, not moving, and said nothing. I don't know if a cold shiver went down my spine but I sat where I was, hardly daring to breathe. I felt as if time had slipped back, in some way, and we were on our first visit here, when Richard had pointed to smoke, and said there was someone there . . .

"Shall we go in?" Kim asked, but we all shook our heads. She didn't seem sorry.

We waited . . .

Then a figure came out on to the porch, smiling, familiar, and an amused voice called across to us, "So you won't answer my smoke-screen?" said Peter Blake. "I saw you coming and I thought the sight of smoke rising mysteriously from the chimney of your favourite ruin would certainly make you rush in and mop up another mystery."

"We haven't mopped this one up yet," Sally said, honestly. She was quicker than the rest of us and said, directly, "That was why you arranged to get us all here this afternoon, wasn't it?"

He laughed and nodded. "I asked your father—and the Judge—if you would be allowed near the inn, *for the last time*! I promised to keep an eagle eye on you."

"No need!" I said. "We've had enough mystery to last until——"

"Until the next?" he finished for me. I had to say I supposed so. (When you are caught up in it, what can you do save help to solve it?)

Obligingly, he sat down facing us, and we listened, without making a stir. We still called him and thought of him as Peter Blake though that wasn't his name, but it was the name we knew and we saw no reason, now, to change it, so late in the day!

He started, with no introductions . . . "Mary Brown had told Livvy part of the truth when she said there was an organisation known as The Silver Circle. A half-truth sometimes sounds as though it carries weight—and it is easier to remember. When one starts on a tissue of *untruths*, even children can pick them out." He looked at me and said, "Sorry, Livvy."

I nodded—so he went on. "Mary Brown thought they would be out of the country very soon. They only meant to stay a short time—long enough to collect the notes and hand them on. That was their job—agents for the organisation. It paid them well—until this last time! It wasn't smuggling, as you know, but counterfeit notes—and Hugh Brown wasn't with the police. On the contrary, we had been anxious to trace him and pin the evidence on him for some time. He was clever—so was his sister —and had eluded us. I knew they were in England but it took me some time to find out just where. They had decided this old inn was a perfect rendez-vous. There was the Common, beyond the woods, where the aeroplane could drop its precious pack-age. That was the plane you heard, Kim. The first night, something had gone wrong. They weren't on time and the plane had to take off. The second night, the package was dropped and picked up. That was the night you so bravely checked up on the number of the car. Don't be surprised—I was there too!"

Kim looked her amazement. She had been so certain she had seen no one.

"I was glad when you went back, though," Peter confessed. "I didn't want anything to happen to you—and what you children never seemed to realise was that these people were *dangerous*."

"They didn't act that way, to us," Sally explained.

"They did to Livvy and Kim," he reminded her.

I nodded and said, "They dropped the notes by parachute—and the Browns buried the parachute? That was what I saw you dig up, in the woods, the afternoon of the Carnival Parade! *Evidence*!"

"That's it." He smiled but I was certain I detected a faint sigh, too. "You have been well and truly mixed up in this, haven't you?"

We had the grace to blush!

"The notes were dropped to the Browns and their job, as I've said, was to distribute them. The members of this organisation were unknown to one another. That way, the head of it—whom we caught before we caught the Browns—thought everything would be safer—for him, most of all! He considered that when his subordinates did not know the names of those above and below them, then, if they were caught, they could give nothing away. We caught them, anyway, but the Browns were almost the last." He paused, evidently thinking over some point known only to himself, and respectfully, we waited. We could have waited all day, if need be!

He went on. "Their only means of identification was a silver ring. That was how they made themselves known to one another. The ring Sally found was Mary Brown's which, by an incredible slip on her part, she had lost at the inn. It wasn't *I* who burgled it—though you don't have to apologise for thinking so. They overheard Richard telling me about it and were there first."

We blushed, again, for our doubts of him. All save Richard, who looked at us, plainly saying, "I told you so—didn't I?"

"*I* already had a ring which we took from one of the others we previously picked up."

(The ring in the drawer in the caravan, I told myself.)

"The member of the gang they were expecting to meet here didn't turn up. He couldn't. We had him. But his place had been taken by Smith, one of our men. Hugh Brown, though, was suspicious. He was always on the alert for danger . . . and so Smith met his 'accident' on the cliff-top."

"The man we found?" Richard asked, and we all sat, looking our amazement at the way we had been well and truly mixed-up in this case. Wherever we went, whatever we did . . .

"That's it. The accident, fortunately, wasn't

fatal and when they saw you and Livvy had discovered their victim, they waited until you were alone, drew your attention elsewhere, then took Smith back, through the cave and passages, and brought him *here*. You'll be glad to know he's safe and sound now. They took him away again, but we got him all right. I think," Peter said, "that fills in the gaps in your story. The end you know, for Kim and Livvy were there." Then, kindly, "What is it, Livvy?"

My face was scarlet but I had to say the words. "All the time," I mumbled, "I trusted Mary Brown. She told me to tell her everything you did —anything that looked suspicious—and I trusted her. I must have spoiled your plans often."

"On the contrary," he said, cheerfully, "you speeded things up. I wasn't alone on the case, of course, and I'm afraid I knew what was happening. I didn't blame you, Livvy, for a moment. They were a plausible pair. I knew they realised we were closing in on them, and it made them nervous and over-hasty. They wanted desperately to get right away from here but had to wait for the plane and dared not leave without the notes. The man in the plane we took, when he landed, later that same night—and if they had got off with the notes, they would have run straight into our arms. They did, anyway, and much *wetter* than they bargained for !

My great worry was that you two—Kim and Livvy —might come to harm!''

"I trusted them too," Sally said. Her face darkened. "And it was Mary Brown who ruined *my* sketch?" She looked across at Kim and, though Sally didn't say anything, I knew she felt like apologising though it is always difficult to apologise for what one has *thought* . . . Kim must have understood for she smiled cheerfully back and now it was *my* turn to think, "I told you so . . ."

"She must have been in the inn, the day I left it on the window-seat—and I was so sure there was no one there!" Sally said.

"She told me herself there were hiding-places no one suspected," I agreed.

"I'm really terribly sorry about that sketch," Peter told Sally. "That was when I knew for certain the Browns were panicking. When that happens, the end is usually near—for they make mistakes, one after the other! They were afraid to let even a sketch of the old place be exhibited, in case it furnished someone—who might be anywhere— with a clue. *Well?*" He looked round. "Any questions—or is that all?"

We thought hard. We shook our heads. No questions.

But . . . "What are you going to do now?" Richard asked.

He meant *the next case,* I know, but, for answer,

Peter Blake showed us the sketch book he carried with him. It was quite new. Admiringly, he looked at it and turned the first page, shining and white. He took out his pencils, newly sharpened. "I was never really satisfied with that first effort," he admitted, "but it gave me the urge for sketching. There were too many distractions, then. Now, I really am on leave! I'm going to sketch the inn, as a souvenir . . ."

I left them there. Peter sketched, with Sally and Kim on each side, giving him so much good advice that at last he tore a sheet for each of them from his sketch-book, handed them a pencil, and told them to get on with it—there would be a prize for the best drawing! Richard sat at his feet, plainly hero-worshipping. To know someone who had seen the Test Matches in Australia was thrilling enough! When this same person turned out to be a real live investigator . . . I could almost *see* Richard making a promise to himself to grow up exactly like Peter Blake.

I wandered into the old inn, through empty, echoing rooms. Nothing here, now, to frighten any-one. By his story, told clearly and simply, Peter Blake had banished for ever what had mystified and frightened us. There were shadows, still, in the corners, but sunshine lay in bars of gold on the floor, and you could hear the birds through the broken windows. The stairs creaked when I walked on them, but now there was no need to look over my shoulder. . . .

I went outside again, where the wild flowers grew beside the front door and ivy over the windows and in through the cracks. . . .

I looked up at the faded sign that creaked above my head. The sun lit it up so that the painted silver circle gleamed as it might have done, the first day it was put up.

THE END